CROW BAIT

Robert J. Randisi

CHIVERS

British Library Cataloguing in Publication Data available

This Large Print edition published by AudioGO Ltd, Bath,
2012.
Published by arrangement with Golden West Literary
Agency

U.K. Hardcover   ISBN 978 1 4458 2360 7
U.K. Softcover   ISBN 978 1 4458 2361 4

Printed and bound in Great Britain by
MPG Books Group Limited

crow bait — an emaciated horse likely to become carrion and so attractive to crows.

ONE

The Mojave Desert, Colorado, 1888

He stared at the sky for a while.

Until he saw one buzzard joined by another, then a third.

Time to move, Lancaster. No time to die.

The problem was, he didn't remember how he had gotten where he was — lying on his back with pain in quite a few parts of his body — especially his head.

Okay, he thought, time to sit up and take stock.

With a groan he worked himself to a seated position, looked around. Nothing but some shrubbery, a few leafless trees, and hard, cracked ground. No other people in sight. The only thing he could see was a dead horse — his horse — lying a few feet away from him. No saddle.

He looked down at himself, checking for bullet wounds. There was some blood but didn't seem to be any holes. His head was

7

pounding, his jaw ached, as did his ribs.

He gave some thought to trying to get to his feet, but his head started to spin so he settled back down on his butt and tried to remember what had happened to put him in this position. . . .

He remembered riding through the Nevada desert on his way to . . . well, where he was going — and to do what — wouldn't come to him. Maybe later. He could have used some water, but he looked around and there was no canteen anywhere . . .

. . . he was riding through the desert, heading somewhere, when suddenly there was a shot and his horse went down. Thinking back, he thought he'd felt the impact of the bullet on the animal beneath him. The horse barely had time to quiver before it went down and died. Luckily, he'd been quick enough to throw himself free before he could become pinned beneath the carcass.

But even as he went for his gun, he was suddenly surrounded by men with their weapons already in their hands. Three men . . .

. . . okay, now it was coming back to him. Without a word the three men attacked him. They could easily have killed him, but instead they began to kick him. All three of them, viciously inflicting pain and damage with their boots. No words, no explanation. At some point his gun had gone flying, and he mercifully lost consciousness . . .

He looked around now, but there was no sight of his pistol or his rifle. He held his head in his hands.

. . . he recalled regaining consciousness while the men were stripping his saddle from his dead horse. They then came to him and took his gun belt, and his boots . . .

His boots? He took his head out of his hands and looked at his feet. No boots, just socks. It was just getting worse.

. . . they rolled him over, went through his pockets, took whatever money was there, then kicked him a few more times for good measure . . .

. . . he woke once more while they were talking, but for some reason he couldn't hear them. And his vision was blurry. He saw . . . something, but couldn't quite figure out what it was.

Then he heard . . .

". . . kill him," someone said. "It would be easier . . . bullet in the head . . ."

"No," someone else said. ". . . not the way . . . supposed to be . . ."

". . . desert will take care . . ."

". . . awake . . ."

They noticed he was awake. He saw one of them step forward and knew another kick was coming, but couldn't do anything to avoid it . . .

Somebody said, "Sweet, don't . . ."

. . . a kick to the head knocked him out . . . again . . .

He sat there, still trying to remember. It came to him in pieces, but the pieces wouldn't fit together. He probed and prodded his body. His jaw hurt, but it didn't appear broken. He couldn't say the same for his ribs. Had to be one or two of them that were cracked. He flexed his arms and legs, found that they worked. Why hadn't they broken one or more of his limbs? That really would have left him in bad shape.

He looked at his feet. Nothing wrong there, except for his toes peeking out of some holes in his socks.

He took a deep breath. It was finally time for him to try getting to his feet.

The first time he almost made it, but his head swam and he staggered, sat back down

Tried again, slowly.

Got to a bent-over position, hands on his knees, then straightened up slowly.

Stood.

Stayed.

It was a start.

Two

The three men rode up to the fourth and dismounted. One of the men — the largest — was carrying an extra saddle. Another man had extra saddlebags. And the third was carrying an extra handgun and rifle.

The man they were meeting was standing next to a buckboard. He was tall, ramrod straight even though he was in his sixties. His face was deeply chiseled with lines he had earned over a long, hard life. And though he currently was a wealthy man, his life was still hard. New lines were still forming.

The man with the saddle walked around and dropped into the bed of the buckboard.

The man with the saddlebags did the same.

The man with the gun walked to the older man and handed them to him.

"Done?" the older man asked.

"Done."

11

The older man handed him an envelope with money in it, payment for all three.

"Do not ever contact me," the older man said.

The man with the envelope looked inside, raised his eyebrows, and said, "You got it."

All three men mounted up and rode off.

The older man with the chiseled face did not move until they were out of sight.

THREE

A step . . .

 . . . then a second . . .

 . . . and a third.

Good, Lancaster, you're almost walking.

Then, when the fourth step came down on a sharp rock, he cried out and sat back down, hard.

"Goddamnit!"

He wasn't going to get far trying to walk in his socks. After a few moments of thought, he decided he could do without the bottom parts of the legs of his jeans. He'd tear them off in strips and wrap them around his feet. That would give him some protection, though probably not as much as even a pair of moccasins.

He was thirsty and beaten up, but was not yet weak. At least, he had the strength to tear his pants legs into strips. By the time he was done, his feet were wrapped and his jeans came down to his knees.

13

Time to try to get to his feet again.

As he put his hands down on the ground to push himself up, he felt something next to him. He looked down and saw that it was his hat. He hadn't noticed it before. At least he'd have that to keep the sun out of his eyes and off his head. He grabbed it and jammed it on.

He repeated the stages, getting his feet beneath him, standing with hands on his knees, and then straightening. He arched his back, winced at the pain in his ribs but did not give in to it. He looked around him. In every direction he saw nothing except an occasional Joshua tree, which was indigenous to the Mojave Desert.

Lancaster knew that the Colorado River was approximately fifty miles to the east. Under normal circumstances — being on horseback — it was an easy ride. On foot it would be more difficult. On foot, with no boots, no water, and having been badly beaten, it would be nearly impossible to get there alive.

But that's what he had to do. The nearest town he knew of was Laughlin. He remembered more now. He had actually been heading to Laughlin when his attackers set upon him. They came riding at him and, being the cautious type, he hadn't hesitated.

He'd kicked his horse into a gallop, rather than stand and draw down on them. In retrospect, he probably should have stood and fought. It's what he would have done in the old days. The rest was still a blur, but he remembered his horse going down and throwing him. Next thing he knew he was being beaten and kicked. . . .

He took a few steps, testing his denim-wrapped feet. It was better — better than socks, certainly better than bare feet.

The sun had long since hit its zenith and was on the way down. He had a few hours of daylight, which was good. He'd last had a drink of water just before the riders came up on him. He wouldn't have to walk in the hot sun for very long. Once it got dark he'd keep walking, make as much time as he could in the dark.

There were four-legged predators he'd have to be careful of — snakes, coyotes, and bobcats. If he ran into any of them, he'd have to be able to defend himself. He'd have to find something — a club, a rock — something he could use if and when the time came.

But he'd have to rest if he was going to make it, and that's when he'd have to watch for insects — spiders and scorpions, mostly.

Resting was far from his mind at the mo-

15

ment, though. What he had to do at the moment was get moving and keep moving. The one thing that could most kill him was if he lost consciousness — and there was good chance of that. He knew he'd been kicked in the head at least a couple of times. His dizziness was not completely gone, but if he gave into it and passed out he knew he might never wake up.

So Lancaster started walking.

FOUR

The horse did not even look fit enough to eat.

The Serrano Indians were not a warlike tribe. The Serranos existed on small game, used them not only for food but clothing, as well. Horses and burros were for riding and work only, so when one of them was no longer fit for that, they turned them loose in the desert.

When Lancaster saw the horse, he couldn't believe it at first. It was just getting dark — he'd only been walking for a couple of hours — and the animal looked like the answer to a prayer — at first.

At second look, the only phrase that came to mind was "crow bait."

He stopped walking and stared.

The animal was standing still, looking completely unconcerned about anything. It was an Indian pony with some mustang throw in, its once straight back slightly

17

bowed, but that wasn't the problem. The problem was all the bones that were showing through its skin.

Its tail swished away flies nonchalantly as it turned its head and stared balefully at Lancaster.

Lancaster stood still and stared at the animal. Dusk had come upon them, and he could already feel the difference in temperature. At night it became much colder in the desert and, if for no other reason, he could use the animal for its warmth.

Now he had to see if he could catch him.

From the pony's appearance, it didn't seem he could run away from Lancaster, but then he wasn't in that great shape himself. From just two hours of walking, even with his feet wrapped, he was sprouting blisters and bleeding from cuts.

"Easy, fella," he said, "easy," as he moved closer.

He needn't have been so careful, though. The horse was making no move to run away. He simply watched as Lancaster came closer.

"There ya go," Lancaster said, reaching his hand out for the horse to sniff.

He let the animal smell his hand for a few moments, then came closer and patted his

18

neck. He then ran his hand over the horse's back and flanks and was appalled at the condition it was in. He was actually afraid that if he got on the horse's back the animal might collapse in a heap of bones.

"Can you walk?" he asked the horse. "Come on." He pushed on the horse's rear flank, and the animal moved. He examined its legs more closely and found them unharmed. Despite its emaciated appearance the horse seemed sound.

Traveling through the desert at night was fairly safe. There were not enough rocks or shrubs to pose a danger, and most of the desert predators were warm-blooded and didn't like the coolness of the night. The only danger was the possibility of your horse stepping in a chuckhole and snapping a leg.

But this was an Indian pony who had spent its life in the desert, surefooted as they came — hopefully.

"Okay," Lancaster said, "I'm gonna try gettin' on your back. You seem tame enough, and I'm in no shape to get thrown, understand?"

Of course, the horse didn't understand. If he threw him, Lancaster didn't know if he'd be able to get up again, but he had to try it. He'd come upon this horse standing in the middle of the desert for a reason.

If he'd had to try this the next day, after a few more hours of walking in the sun, he probably would not have been able to climb aboard, but he still had some strength left. Despite the pain in his sides from being kicked, he managed to drag himself up onto the horse's back. He sat there a moment, catching his breath, waiting tensely for the horse to buck.

It didn't.

Lancaster leaned over and patted the horse's neck

"You and me are gonna get along fine."

The horse's head went up and down, as if in agreement.

"Now let's see if you can walk."

He gigged the horse with his sore feet and the animal did indeed begin to walk. Granted, he walked very slowly, but at least they were moving, and in the right direction.

"You know where the river is, too, don't you?" Lancaster asked.

The horse just kept walking.

"Well, if you and me are gonna spend some time together," Lancaster said, "and depend on each other, I think I need to be able to call you something other than horse."

They rode for a while, Lancaster trying to

come up with a likely name. Finally he did, but it was chancy.

"You might throw me when I tell you this," he said, "but I think I'm gonna call you Crow Bait."

He tensed, but nothing happened. The horse just kept walking.

"Okay, then," Lancaster said, "Crow Bait it is."

FIVE

Crow Bait walked until morning, and would have walked farther if Lancaster had allowed him.

"Where are you getting this from?" Lancaster asked the horse, stroking his neck. "You're a bag of skin and bones, and yet you keep going."

Lancaster didn't dare get down off the horse. He wasn't sure he'd be able to get back up again. He had drifted off a couple of times during the night, either to sleep or unconsciousness, he wasn't sure which. But he had awakened in time to keep himself from slipping off Crow Bait's back.

The sun was coming up, and while there were still a few Joshua trees around, they did not afford much in the way of shade. There was no point in stopping. He and the horse might not have been able to start again.

"I don't mean to ride you to death, boy,"

he said apologetically, "but I don't have much choice. And you look like you're pretty near death, anyway."

But as near death as he might have been, the horse went on.

If Lancaster had been a religious man, he might have thought that this animal was something supernatural sent to him to save him. But he wasn't religious — not ever, and he didn't intend to start now.

"But whoever sent you to me," he said to Crow Bait, "I'd sure like to thank them in person someday. That is, if you and me manage to get out of this alive."

Lancaster opened his eyes and squinted as the sun burned into them. He'd done it again, fallen asleep or lost consciousness. His mouth was dry, and his skin felt like sand.

He pulled his hat down low on his head to shield his eyes and then tried opening them again. He was still on the horse, and Crow Bait was still walking.

"Headin' toward water, boy?" he asked. His throat was so dry he didn't think the words had come out. He'd just heard them in his head.

Only the smell of water could have kept Crow Bait walking the way he was. As long as he didn't fall off the horse's back during one of his blackouts, if Crow Bait made it to water, so would he.

He hoped he'd be awake when they got there.

Six

Lancaster opened his eyes and flinched at the expected glare of the sun, only it wasn't there. He frowned, stared straight up. There was no sun, and no sky. He was staring at a ceiling.

And he was lying on something soft and smooth.

He moved his hands in front of his eyes, to make sure he was seeing right. He flexed his fingers, then touched his face.

"Oh, good," somebody said, "you're awake."

"Wha—" he said, but the word wouldn't come out. He turned his head and saw a woman standing in a doorway. Then he looked around, saw that he was in a room with walls, and a ceiling and furniture. He put his hands down, felt the sheets and the bed beneath him.

"I — I —" He tried to speak, but the words wouldn't come out.

"How about some water?" the woman said. She came to the bed, held his head, and tipped a glass to his dry lips. The water trickled down his throat and felt good.

"There," the woman said, setting his head back on the pillow.

"I — is this real?" he asked, his voice raspy.

"Oh yes," she said, "this is very real. You're in my house, and you're safe."

He took a deep breath, looked around again, and looked at her. She was somewhere between a woman and a girl — mid-twenties, maybe.

"Your house?"

"My family's house," she said. "My brothers and me."

"How — when —"

"Just relax," she said. "Your horse came walkin' up to the house with you unconscious on its back. My brothers caught you as you fell off, and we brought you inside. You're safe."

"How — what kind of shape —"

"Are you in?" she finished. "Well, your feet have cuts and blisters on them, and you were kinda dried out from being in the sun. Also, somebody seems to have put the boots to you. Your body's a mass of bruises, and your face. But other than that, nothin' seems to be broke."

26

"Tha-that's good," he stammered, "but I was going to ask you about my — my horse."

"Oh, the horse?" she asked, laughing. "That wasn't much of a horse, mister. It's amazing he got you here. My older brother, Ben, wanted to put a bullet between the poor animal's eyes, but —"

"No!" Lancaster said. "He can't!" He tried to sit up, but she stopped him.

"No, no, it's okay," she said. "I didn't let him. The horse is fine. He's in the barn. Just . . . lie back."

Lancaster allowed her to push him back down.

"You need some more water," she said, "and you need some food."

"How long have I been here?" he asked.

"Since yesterday." She held the water for him again, and he took more this time.

"My horse," he said. "Water . . . did you give him water . . . feed . . . ?"

"He's been watered, fed, rubbed down, and fed again," she said. "Don't worry."

"That animal saved my life," he said. "I was on foot, and then he was there . . ."

"Mister, nobody's gonna hurt your horse, I promise."

"Okay," he said, "okay." He took a deep breath.

27

"Are you hungry?" she asked.

"Actually," he said, "now that I think about it . . . yes."

"I'm makin' dinner for me and my brothers," she said. "I can bring a tray in here — unless you think you can walk?"

"Uh, I don't know," he said. "I could try."

"Well," she said, "why don't we try standin' first, and go from there?"

"Why not?" Lancaster said.

She removed the sheet and blanket to allow him to stand. He swung his legs around, put his feet down, and hesitated. Someone — presumably the woman — had bandaged the cuts and blisters on his feet.

"Go ahead," she said. "Try."

He nodded, put his weight on his feet for a moment, and stood up.

"Whoa," she said as he swayed. "Dizzy?"

"A little."

"You really should have a doctor look at you," she said.

"How far are we from the nearest town?"

"About eight miles from Laughlin."

"We made it that far?"

"How far?"

"Maybe fifty miles or so."

"On that horse? That's amazing. All right, do you want to try walking?"

"That would be the logical next step,

28

wouldn't it?" he said, words coming a bit easier now.

He took a step.

SEVEN

With her help he made it to the kitchen, where two men were sitting at the table. They watched as he made his way across the floor and she helped him to sit.

"Boys, this is Mr. —"

"Lancaster."

"Mr. Lancaster," she said. "My name is Kimmie, that's my brother Zack, and that's our brother Ryan."

"How do," Ryan said. He looked like the younger of the two brothers.

"We're waitin' on supper, Kimmie," Zack said.

"It's comin', Zack," she said. "Be polite to our guest."

Zack looked across the table at Lancaster. "You on the run?"

"What does that mean, exactly?" Lancaster asked.

"I mean, is the law after you?"

"No."

"But somebody is."

"Not exactly."

"Then what, exactly?"

Kimmie came over and put a plate of food and a cup of coffee in front of him. "Zack, that ain't exactly bein' polite, is it?"

"I'm just lookin' out for my family," Zack said. "I gotta know who we got under our roof."

"That's fair," Lancaster said.

Kimmie went back to the stove.

"I was ambushed out in the desert," Lancaster said. "Three men rode me down. My horse took a fall. They beat me senseless, stole everything I had, left me to die out there."

"And that horse you rode in on?" Zack asked.

"Found it."

"You took a chance gettin' up on that bag of bones," Ryan said.

Kimmie put plates in front of her brothers and then sat down with one for herself.

"He got me here, didn't he?" Lancaster asked. "He was — I was amazed. He just . . . kept going."

"The way he looks," Zack said, "a bullet would be a blessin'."

"No," Lancaster said, "he just needs some care."

31

Lancaster put some stew in his mouth. It was the best thing he'd ever tasted, and he wasn't sure it was because he had just come off the desert.

"This is great," he said.

"Probably because you ain't et in a while," Ryan said, with a grin at his sister.

"Shut up and eat, Ryan," she said, grinning back at him.

"You gonna go after the men who waylaid you?" Zack asked.

"I plan to."

"On that horse?"

"I don't know," Lancaster said. "When I'm ready I'll see if he's ready. Can you take me into Laughlin? I can rest up there, get outfitted —"

"You got any money?" Kimmie asked.

Lancaster looked at her.

"You said they stole everythin'."

"No," he said, "I have no money."

"Then how will you get outfitted?" she asked. "You'll need a horse and a gun."

"I have a horse," Lancaster said.

"We can loan you a better one," she said, "and a gun. A rifle, anyway."

"Now, hold on —" Zack said.

"A ride to town is all I really need," Lancaster said, not wanting to cause dissension in their family.

32

"Nonsense," she said. "You're in no shape to ride to town."

"You said I should see a doctor."

"I can care for you for a few days," Kimmie said. "When you're strong enough the boys can take you to town and you can see the doc."

"Kimmie's a frustrated mom," Ryan said. "Always motherin' us, and now you're in fer it."

"Hasn't hurt him so far," she said.

"And it won't," Lancaster said, "if I can get another bowl of this stew."

"Comin' up," she said.

"We only got his word that he ain't on the run from the law," Zack said. "I think we should take him to town tomorrow."

Kimmie brought Lancaster another bowl.

"You'll have to forgive Zack," she said. "Since Papa died he's been trying to fill his shoes. Usually he does a pretty good job, but sometimes he's just downright rude."

"Ain't rude to try to protect my family," Zack said.

"He's right," Lancaster said.

"Well," Kimmie said, sitting back down, "I believe your story. I don't think the law would've left you afoot in the desert."

"Kimmie's got a point, Zack," Ryan said.

"Shut up and eat, Ryan," Zack said.

EIGHT

After supper Kimmie offered to walk Lancaster back to bed, but he asked her to walk him outside instead. When they got out to the porch she sat him down in a wooden rocking chair.

"Used to be Papa's," she said.

Lancaster looked around. They didn't have much beyond the house, just a barn and an empty corral.

"It ain't much," she said, sitting next to him in a straight-backed chair.

He looked at her. She was wearing a simple cotton dress that looked homemade, long brown hair pulled back in a ponytail. Her face was weathered, but didn't make her look old. She just looked like she spent a lot of time outdoors. Over the years, though, it would eat away at her looks.

"I don't want to cause trouble between you and your brother," he said.

"No trouble," she said. "You'll need a

34

couple of days before you can put your feet into a pair of boots. I have a pair of Papa's that might fit you. Also some clothes."

"You're very kind, Kimmie," he said.

"You're just somebody in need," she said. "I can't very well turn you away."

"Yeah, but not a lot of people would offer me clothes, and a bed, and a rifle. . . ."

"Then you ain't been meetin' the right kind of people, Mr. Lancaster."

"Just Lancaster," he said. "No Mister, and you're right. I haven't met the right kind of people. At least, not people like you."

"You just sit here a while and relax," she said, standing up. "I'll bring you some coffee and a piece of pie."

As she went in, Zack came out, with Ryan in tow.

"We still got some daylight to work by," he said to Kimmie.

"What about pie?" she asked.

"After we're done," he said. He looked at Lancaster, then walked away, yanking his brother by the sleeve.

Lancaster watched as the brothers crossed to the barn and went inside. Whatever work they had, it was in there, because they didn't come back out.

In the barn Ryan asked, "What are we

35

gonna do about Lancaster?"

"What about him?"

"Kimmie wants him to stay until he's better."

"Even if we let him," Zack said, "it'll only be for a few days at most."

"And then we have to take him into town?" Ryan asked, worried.

"Ryan, take it easy," Zack said, putting his hand on his brother's shoulder. "We've never robbed the bank in Laughlin. Nobody there is gonna be lookin' for us. That's why we don't hit banks close to home."

"You're pretty smart, Zack," Ryan said.

"Yeah, I'm real smart," Zack said. "That's why our little sister is wasting away out here in the desert."

"Hey, it's like you keep sayin'," Ryan said. "As soon as we have enough money, we'll all get outta here."

"Yeah," Zack said, "right. Okay, let's fix the axle on this buckboard. We'll need it to take Lancaster to Laughlin."

Kimmie came out with a slice of apple pie and another cup of coffee.

"So," she asked, "will you stay?"

"A couple of days," he said, "if you can get Zack to stop giving me the evil eye."

"I can handle Zack," she said. "He's the

big brother, I'm the little sister. I can usually get what I want."

"Okay, then a couple of days," he said. "That'll give me time to look over Crow Bait and see how he is."

"Crow Bait?"

"That's what I decided to call him."

She clapped her hands and said, "How wonderful! What a perfect name."

He tried the pie and found it very tasty.

"Tell me, Kimmie, what kind of operation do you have here?"

"It's not much now," she said. "When Papa started it he was raising cattle and growing wild meadow hay. He always said we had the desert behind us, but a lot of fertile land in front of us."

"So what do your brothers do?"

"They work odd jobs on other ranches, or in Laughlin. Zack thinks that someday he'll be able to bring Papa's ranch back to what it was. . . ."

"You don't agree?"

"No," she said. "I want to leave this place."

"Can you get your brothers to sell it?"

"Ryan, maybe, but not Zack. That's one thing I can't get him to do."

"So why don't you just leave? How old are you?"

"I'm nineteen."

37

So maybe the weathered condition of her face did add some years. He had guessed her at about twenty-five. There was time for her to reverse the effects, though, if she could get away from this life.

"You have time, then."

She smiled and said, "Not as much as I'd like. I saw your face when I told you how old I was. I know I look older. And I'll look older every year that I live here. Unless . . ."

"Unless?"

"Unless you take me with you when you leave," she said, grabbing his arm.

"Oh, Kimmie," he said, "I'll barely be able to take care of myself when I leave here — and I'm only going to Laughlin. You've been to Laughlin —"

"No," she said, "I haven't."

He stared at her.

"It's eight miles away," he said. "You've never been there?"

"Well, when I was a little girl, but I haven't ever had any reason to go in years," she said. "The boys go in for supplies, or to do some jobs. I stay home and . . . keep house." She shrugged. "I'm the mother. My brothers think I like it, but I don't."

"You'll make a great mother," Lancaster said, "but for some of your own kids, not your brothers."

"How will I ever get married and have my own children," she asked, "if I can't get away from here? Unless . . ." She grabbed his arm again.

"I'm a little old for you, Kimmie," he said, "and I'm not the marrying kind."

"I guess I'm stuck here, then."

"Why don't you just insist that your brothers take you along next time they go to town?" he asked. "Maybe when they take me in?"

"I suppose I could try to insist," she said, "but Zack always says somebody has to stay home."

"Well, you've got a couple of days," Lancaster said. "Work on him."

NINE

After a good night's sleep and an even better breakfast the next morning, Lancaster pulled on the borrowed boots that used to belong to Kimmie's father. He stood up, found that they fit pretty well, even though his feet still hurt a bit. The shirt and trousers she had given him were a little small, but not noticeably.

Lancaster left the house and walked over to the barn. He hadn't gotten much out of Kimmie's brothers that morning, except some borderline hostile look from Zack. But Kimmie appeared to have gotten her way, and the brothers were prepared to take him to Laughlin in two or three days.

In the barn he found Crow Bait standing easily, chewing on some hay. As he entered, the animal turned his head and gave him a stare, then looked away.

There were four other horses in the barn — two saddle mounts and a team to pull the buckboard. They were all eight years old or more, but sound.

Lancaster was shocked at Crow Bait's appearance. He'd forgotten how truly bad he looked.

"Wow," he said, touching the animal's flank, "you really do look like crow bait."

He examined the horse, running his hands over him. Aside from seeming frail and knock-kneed, the legs seemed sound enough. His neck seemed too long for his body, and too slender to carry a large head. Lancaster figured that a few weeks of eating regularly would fill that out, make the head and neck look more in proportion. The same with all the bones that seemed to be sticking out here and there. Some extra flesh would smooth them out.

He brushed Crow Bait while the horse continued to chew. His coat was spotty, seemingly worn away in some places, but the flesh beneath seemed unmarked. They could have been just bald spots, and he wondered if the hair there would grow back. Likewise, the tail was thin and ragged. He didn't know if that would fill back in or not with a steady diet.

"You saved my life," Lancaster said, stroking the horse's neck, "so I'm gonna see that you get to live yours."

By checking the horse's mouth and teeth, he surmised him to be five or six years old.

"You've got plenty of life ahead of you, boy," Lancaster said. "You're gonna be well taken care of."

Crow Bait, unconcerned with his appearance, continued to feed.

TEN

At supper the night before they were to take Lancaster to Laughlin Kimmie said, "Zack, I wanna come with you tomorrow."

"No."

"You can't just say no," she said.

"Why do you want to go to town?" he asked. "You ain't never been to town."

"I been when I was a little girl, but I ain't been in a long time, and I wanna go."

"You gotta stay here," Zack said.

"Why?"

"Somebody's gotta stay home," he said.

"Why?" she asked again.

Zack gave Lancaster a hard stare.

"This your doin'?" he demanded.

"Me? I've got nothing to do with it."

"Don't you dare blame him," Kimmie said, her eyes flashing. "I'm tired of just stayin' here all the time, alone, while you and Ryan go off and do God knows what."

"We're workin' when we go away," Zack

said. "You think we're out there havin' fun?"

"You can't be workin' all the time!" she argued. "You got to be havin' fun sometime."

She looked at Ryan, who ducked his head and looked away.

"What if some other drifter drags his ass here lookin' for help?" Zack asked.

"He'll hafta help himself," Kimmie said. "I'm comin' to town!"

Zack stared at her. He must have seen something in her face that made him say, "Fine, you can come."

"I can?"

"You ain't gonna gimme a minute's peace until I say yes, right?" Zack asked.

"Right."

"Then get me some more supper and we can stop talkin' about it."

She went to the stove happily, while Zack continued to stare at Lancaster unhappily.

"I'm telling you, I had nothing to do with this," he said again.

Ryan found it funny, but Zack continued to scowl as Kimmie gave him a second helping.

The next morning the brothers hooked the team up to the buckboard, then saddled their mounts. Lancaster and Kimmie climbed into the seat of the buckboard, and — with Crow Bait tied to the back of the buckboard — they left for Laughlin.

Laughlin was bustling when they arrived. There were ruts in the road from the constant traffic. A couple of times the buckboard wheels got crossways of a rut and rattled Lancaster's ribs.

"Sorry," Kimmie said.

"Don't worry about it."

"I'm gonna drop you in front of the doctor's office," she said. "That is, if it's where I remember it bein'."

"I don't have the money to pay a doctor," he said. "Just drop me in front of the hotel."

"If you can't pay the doc, how do you plan to pay for a hotel room?"

"I'm supposed to have a job waiting here for me," Lancaster said. "I'm late, but maybe it's still waiting. I can get an advance."

"Then you can see Doc," she said. "He's a nice old fella who comes out by us a lot. He'll wait for his money. And we'll drop your horse at the livery for ya."

"Okay, then," Lancaster said. "The doctor's."

"Ribs ain't broke," Dr. Murphy said, "but

45

they're sure as hell sore. Put your shirt back on."

As Lancaster donned his borrowed shirt, the doctor looked at his feet.

"Cuts and blisters. The cut over your eye may scar, but somebody cleaned 'em real well."

"A girl named Kimmie."

"Kimmie Castle?" the doctor said.

"I guess," Lancaster said. "Is there another girl with two brothers named Ryan and Zack?"

"Nope," the doctor said, "them's the Castle family, all right."

"Well, my horse carried me to their ranch, and they took me in for a few days."

The doctor chuckled. "Bet Zack wasn't happy about that."

"He wasn't, but Kimmie got her way."

The doctor laughed again, shaking his head. "She usually does."

The doctor looked into Lancaster's eyes.

"Kicks to the head don't seem to have done much damage," he said. "You got a hard head, boy?"

"Pretty hard."

"Guess that saved ya," the older man said. "You seem okay to me. Pull your boots back on and come into my office."

Lancaster pulled on the boots and got to

his feet, limped a bit as he walked into the doctor's office.

"What about my memory?" he asked the doctor.

"It's patchy, right?"

"Yeah."

"That's from being kicked in the head," Murphy said. "It should come back."

"Should?"

"Might."

"I liked should better."

"We don't know that much about these kinds of injuries, Mr. Lancaster," the doctor said. "Your memory of the incident should return."

"Okay."

"I suspect, since you told me you were robbed, that you don't have the money to pay me."

"I have a job waiting for me in town," Lancaster said. "I'll pay you as soon as I check in and get paid. Kimmie assured me that you'd wait."

"I'm used to waitin' for my money, Mr. Lancaster," the doctor said. "Here's my bill, you pay me when you can."

"Thanks, Doc," Lancaster said, accepting the bill and putting it in his pocket. "I'll pay it as soon as I can."

The doctor waved, and Lancaster left the office.

ELEVEN

Lancaster left the doctor's office and went right to the local Wells Fargo office. As he entered, the burly man seated at the desk looked up and raised bushy eyebrows.

"Well, you made it," he said.

"Just barely."

"Have a seat," the Wells Fargo man said. "You don't look so good."

"I don't feel so good." Lancaster extended his hand to the man, who shook it. Then he took a seat.

"What happened?" Andy Black asked.

Lancaster told his friend the story, right up to the visit to the doctor's office.

"So you're okay?" Andy asked.

"I'll be okay," Lancaster said, "as soon as I catch up to the sons of bitches who left me for dead."

"Did you see them? Know who they are?"

"My memory of the event is sketchy," Lancaster said. "But I'll get it back. First

49

I've got to get outfitted. If I could get some pay in advance —"

"Lancaster," Andy said, sitting back and placing his hand on his ample belly, "I'm sorry, but when you didn't show up I had to give the job to someone else."

That wasn't what Lancaster wanted to hear. He was only in Laughlin because Andy Black had asked him to come to do a job for Wells Fargo. But he had to understand.

"Okay, Andy," he said, pushing slowly to his feet. "I understand."

"I'm really sorry, Lancaster." Andy stood up and reached out to his friend.

"Forget it, Andy," Lancaster said, heading for the door.

"Hey, wait, wait," Andy said, coming around his desk. "How you gonna get outfitted, or even get a hotel room? You got a horse?"

"The same one that carried me out of the desert."

"I thought you said he was crow bait?"

"I said that was his name," Lancaster said.

"Look, Lancaster," Andy said, "wait a minute."

He went behind his desk to the Wells Fargo safe, opened it, and took out a steel lockbox.

"I don't need a handout, Andy," Lancaster said.

"This ain't a handout, Lancaster," Andy said. "At least let me cover your expenses. You're only here because of me."

He came around the desk. "Here's enough to pay your doctor bill, a meal, and some clothes."

"Thanks, Andy." Lancaster accepted the money.

"And we keep a couple of hotel rooms at the Laughlin House Hotel for when some Wells Fargo personnel come to town. I can let you have one of those rooms for as long as you stay — that is, as long as none of my bosses come to town."

"I really appreciate this, Andy," Lancaster said. "I'll pay you back."

"It's company money," Andy said. "I'm sure you'll be workin' for us at some point soon. So why don't we just go ahead and call it an advance, like you asked for in the first place?"

Lancaster shook his friend's hand and said, "Agreed."

"Meet me here after five and I'll buy you a steak," Andy said. "We can catch up — or talk about how you can find those three bastards."

"Okay, I'll be here."

"I'll send a message over to the hotel now," Andy said. "Your room will be waitin' when you get there."

Lancaster nodded his thanks and left the office.

After paying his doctor bill — to the surprise of the doctor — he went and checked in at the Laughlin House. True to Andy's word, a room was waiting for him. In fact, it was a two-room suite, which was more than he needed.

What he needed was a bath, and some new clothes. After that, a meal with Andy, and maybe some conversation that might bring his memory back into focus.

And he had to see about Crow Bait. He decided to do that first.

He found the livery and told the man he was there about the Indian pony.

"That crow bait?" the man asked. "You the crazy man who's payin' for that horse to take up one of my stalls?"

"I'm the crazy man," Lancaster said. "I want him well fed and cared for. I want to put some weight back on him. Understand?"

"I understand," the man said, "but I don't

52

know why. It'll take more than some weight
—"

"How much?" Lancaster asked.

"How long you gonna be in town?"

"A few days, maybe."

"Gimme three dollars for now."

Lancaster gave him the money.

"My name's Mal. I'll take good care of
him, but I don't know how much good it
will do."

"My name is Lancaster, and I guess we'll
just have to wait and see."

He had a bath, then bought some new
clothes, but he spent the money Andy Black
had given him sparingly. One shirt, one pair
of trousers, one pair of boots, socks, and
underwear.

"I'll need a saddle," he told the clerk.
"Where can I get one in town?"

"A good one?"

"A good used one."

"Is your horse at the livery?"

"Yes."

"Then that's where I'd get the saddle."

"That's what I thought," Lancaster said.
"Thanks."

He left the general store, wearing all of his
new clothes — except for the hat, which
was the same one he'd been wearing in the
desert. A new one could come later.

He walked over to the Wells Fargo office at five minutes to five.

TWELVE

Andy Black took Lancaster to a steak house a few streets away and ordered two steak dinners with everything.

"Eat up," he said. "Your horse isn't the only one who needs to eat."

"I was only in the desert for a couple of days," Lancaster said. "I was beaten, but not starved."

"And you were at the Castle place for a few days," Andy said. "I bet you lost a little weight."

"Kimmie Castle is a great cook," Lancaster said. "I don't think so."

"Kimmie Castle," Andy said. "Haven't seen her in a long time. Still pretty?"

"Very."

"And her brothers?"

"Not so pretty. Zack wasn't happy that she was nursing me back to health."

"Zack's never happy," Andy said. "They in town?"

"They all brought me here."

"All of them? Her, too?"

"Yes."

"Well, that's an event."

The waiter brought the steak dinners and they each dug in. Andy ate as ravenously as Lancaster did.

Halfway through Andy said, "How's your memory?"

Lancaster frowned. "Three men rode me down. Shot my horse. Before I knew it, they were on me, putting the boots to me. I went in and out of consciousness. Whenever I came to they knocked me out again."

"See anything? Faces?"

"No."

"Anything at all?"

"Boots," Lancaster said. "And I heard voices."

"Saying?"

Lancaster frowned again. "I think I heard one saying they should kill me, and another saying . . ."

"What?"

"That wasn't the plan."

"What plan?"

"I don't know that," Lancaster said.

"So they were paid to ambush you and leave you in the desert to die?"

"That's how it sounded," Lancaster said.

56

"So," Andy said, "all you need is to think of who wants you dead that badly."

"That much I can remember."

"Good. Who?"

Lancaster took a bite of potato and said, "Lots of people."

After supper Andy Black went home to a small house he had on the edge of town. No wife. He was married to his job. He didn't gamble, didn't drink excessively. And he liked his time alone.

Lancaster decided to go and see the local sheriff. Maybe if he talked out his attack with the law, one of them would come up with something.

He found the sheriff's office and entered without knocking because the door was unlocked. The room was odd, L-shaped, with a desk to his right. At the end of the shorter stretch of the room was a door to the cell blocks. The man seated behind the desk looked up at him with interest.

"Help ya?" he asked.

"Sheriff?"

"That's right." The man straightened in his chair, bringing the badge pinned to his chest into view. "Sheriff Harlan Race."

"My name's Lancaster. I just came to town today. I was supposed to be doing a job for Wells Fargo, but I got waylaid in the desert on the way here and left for dead."

The sheriff pointed to the chair opposite him and said, "Have a seat and tell me about it."

Lancaster sat down and started talking.

"Three men, you said?" the sheriff asked when Lancaster finished.

"That's right."

"And you didn't see their faces?"

"Not that I can remember," Lancaster said. "The doc says my memory of the incident should come back, and maybe it is, but it's still got . . . holes."

"So you might've seen their faces and don't remember?" the sheriff asked.

"No," Lancaster said. "I don't think I ever saw their faces clearly."

"What did you see?"

"Boots," Lancaster said. "Mostly boots."

"Anythin' about them you can remember?"

Lancaster thought for a moment, tried to bring back into focus the boots that were inflicting pain on him.

"What?" the sheriff asked. "What's that look?"

"Something . . ." Lancaster said. "Something about the boots."

58

"What?"

"I don't know," he said. "The stitching, maybe?"

"Somethin' . . . distinctive?"

"Maybe," Lancaster said. "I'm not sure." Suddenly, he had a brutal headache.

"You okay?" the sheriff asked.

"Headache. I'll be okay. Were there any strangers in town last week?"

"A few," Race said. "I didn't see three together, though."

"Maybe they stayed away from each other," Lancaster said, "didn't want to be seen together."

"Maybe," Race said. "Let me think about it. Where are you stayin'?"

"The Laughlin House."

"Okay, if I think of anything I'll let you know."

"Okay, thanks."

"Lancaster," the sheriff said as he started to leave.

"Yes?"

"Are you plannin' on hunting for these men?"

"That's the general idea," Lancaster said. "If I can somehow figure out who they are — or, at least, who one of them is."

"From their boots?"

"From something," Lancaster said. "Anything."

"A man's boots, that's not much to base killing him on."

"Hopefully," Lancaster said, "I'll have more to go on."

Thirteen

When Lancaster left the sheriff's office, he was thinking about boots. The voice calling him from behind startled him. He turned, his hand going for his gun, but he didn't have one. He was going to have to remedy that next. Should have asked Andy Black for the loan of one.

"I been lookin' for you," Kimmie said. "Where ya been?"

"Taking care of some business," he said. "You and your brothers are still in town, huh?"

"Sure are," she said. "Gonna head back in about an hour."

"You're going back?"

"Well, sure," she said. "I mean, I know what I said, but it's my home, and they're my brothers."

"I guess you're right."

They started to walk together.

"You look better," she said. "New clothes,

61

a bath. What'd the doc say?"

"He said you did a good job of nursing me back to health," Lancaster said. "He said I should start remembering more and more about the attack."

"That's good, right?"

"He said I should start remembering," Lancaster said, "not that I will."

"Have you remembered anything yet?"

"Just bits and pieces," he said. "Nothing that I can put together."

"Where are you goin' now?"

"I've got to find a gun," Lancaster said, "a cheap gun."

"Didn't you get that advance you wanted from your job?"

"The job wasn't there," Lancaster said, "but I did get some expense money. Enough for some clothes, maybe a cheap saddle and a cheap gun."

"There's a rifle in the buckboard," she said. "I brought it in case you needed it."

He stopped walking.

"That was real thoughtful of you, Kimmie," he said. "I should pick it up before you leave."

"Okay," she said. "The buckboard's in front of the general store. Follow me."

He did.

■ ■ ■ ■

It was an old Henry, but it was in working order — or would be when he cleaned it.

"Shells?" he asked.

"It's loaded," she said, "but I didn't have any more shells."

"Okay, Kimmie, thanks," he said. "Where are Zack and Ryan?"

"Inside."

"Zack know about this?"

"He won't care," she said. "He never touches that rifle."

"Okay," Lancaster said, "thanks, Kimmie, for everything. I don't know when I'll be able to repay you . . . or even if . . ."

"Someday, you will," she said. "We'll just wait and see."

They shook hands awkwardly. He sensed she wanted more, but he didn't have any more to give.

"Bye, Kimmie," he said.

"Good-bye, Lancaster," she said. "See you around, huh?"

FOURTEEN

Lancaster felt better walking the streets with
the rifle in his hand, even though he wasn't
sure it would fire in its present condition.
But he also needed a pistol and a holster. If
the liveryman was the man to see for a used
saddle, maybe he knew where to get a used
handgun, as well. Or maybe Andy Black
knew, but he was home and probably
wouldn't want to be disturbed.

He went to the livery, and actually found
the man brushing Crow Bait.

"Told you I'd look out for him," he said.
"You didn't have to come back and check."

"I'm not checking," Lancaster said.
"What's your full name?"

"Just Mal," the man said. "What's yours?"

"Lancaster. You only got one name?"

The man grinned, showed some gaps
where there used to be teeth. "Men get to
be our age, you realize one name's enough,
right?"

"Okay."

"What can I do for you?"

"I'm gonna need a rig," Lancaster said. "Saddle, saddlebags."

"New I can't help ya with, but used . . ."

"Used is good."

"We can talk."

"I also need a gun."

Mal looked at the rifle in his hand.

"A handgun," Lancaster said, "and holster."

"New or used?"

"Can't afford new."

"We can talk."

Lancaster looked around. "Got 'em here?"

"Let's go in the office," Mal said.

"Lead the way."

Lancaster liked the way Mal stroked Crow Bait's neck before walking away from him.

Mal led him to a door in the back, which led to a small office with a rolltop desk and a trunk. In one corner were three saddles, stacked.

"Sometimes folks don't come back for their stuff," Mal said. "Or they don't pay their bill. Take your pick."

Lancaster walked to the saddles, separated them, and examined them. "This one looks like it'll hold together. How much?"

"Well," Mal said, "it's just sittin' there get-

65

tin' dusty . . . Twenty dollars?"

"With saddlebags?"

Mal walked to the chest, opened it, and pulled a worn pair of saddlebags. "Twenty-two, with the saddlebags."

"Deal."

Mal tossed the bags to him.

"Now how about that gun?"

Again, Mal reached into the trunk, came up with a rolled-up holster with a walnut grip of a pistol showing. He tossed it over. Lancaster deftly caught it, unrolled the leather. It was a Peacemaker with a worn grip, but it was generally clean and well cared for. So was the holster.

"Somebody's been oiling this leather," Lancaster said.

"The gun used to be mine," Mal said. "I take care of it when I can."

Lancaster took it, checked the action on it, spun the cylinder. "How much?"

"A hundred?"

"I don't have a hundred."

"A hundred for everything," Mal said. "Saddle, saddlebags, and gun. But you gotta bring the gun back when you're done."

Lancaster took out the money he had left. "I have sixty dollars left. Then I'm broke."

"You really need that gun, right?" Mal asked. "Rifle ain't enough?"

"I really need the gun."

"I tell you what," Mal said. "Take it all, but when you're done you gotta bring it all back."

"Are you serious?"

"Except for one thing."

"What's that?"

"I want the horse, too."

"Crow Bait? Why?"

"I'm already fond of him."

"What's the real reason?"

Mal scratched his nose.

"I recognize your name," he said finally. "You and me, we used to be in the same business."

"What business is that?"

"The business that requires a handgun."

"I'm not in that business anymore."

Mal spread his arms and said, "Neither am I, as you can see. But you need a gun for somethin', and I know the feelin'. So take it all, but bring it all back when you're done."

"You're serious."

"I'm serious."

Lancaster looked around at everything, then said, "Thanks."

"I'll get back to your horse now."

"Your horse," Lancaster said. "I'm just borrowing it."

67

"I forgot," Mal said. "I'll get the saddle in better shape for you. Gun, too, if you want."

"I'll work on the gun myself," Lancaster said. "Thanks."

They walked back out to Crow Bait, and Mal picked up the brush.

"I hope you get 'em," he said.

"Get who?"

"Whoever gave you that limp, and the cuts and bruises," Mal said.

Lancaster strapped the holster on, slid the gun in and out a few times before settling it back in.

"Feel better?" Mal asked.

"Yeah," Lancaster said, "suddenly, I'm feeling a lot better."

FIFTEEN

Lancaster was thinking that since his last kick in the head his luck had turned. He'd found Crow Bait, who had taken him to Kimmie, who had driven him to town. His job wasn't waiting for him, but Andy staked him to enough money to get him outfitted, and gave him a hotel room. Then he met Mal, who loaned him the rest of what he needed.

Now he needed a drink.

He went to his room to drop off the gun belt and gun. The rifle he kept with him as he walked to the K.O. Saloon as it was getting dark outside. The place was busy, but there were open spaces at the bar, so he claimed one.

"What can I getcha?" the bartender asked. He was big, brawny, had the body and the face of an old prizefighter, which probably explained the name of the place.

"Beer," Lancaster said, "nice and cold."

The bartender laughed. "Only kind we sell, friend."

He placed the cold beer in front of Lancaster.

"How about a shot of whiskey to go with it?" the man asked.

"No, thanks," Lancaster said. It wasn't so long ago that he had crawled into a bottle, and crawled out again. He wasn't about to start that slide all over again. A cold beer once in a while, that was all.

Lancaster lingered over that one beer, trying to pull his thoughts — or his memories — together. Boots, he remembered boots. But what stood out about them? And what else was there? He'd gone in and out of consciousness. Had heard voices. Seen figures. Had he seen faces and was just not remembering them?

Suddenly, he grew very tired. He finished off the beer, staggered back to his hotel, fell onto the bed fully dressed, and slept fitfully.

In the morning he woke with a pounding headache. All night he'd had dreams. He was being chased, being beaten, and he heard voices — only were they dreams? Or was his brain trying to remember things?

He decided to skip breakfast and go see

the doctor. Maybe the doc could give him something for the headache and Lancaster could also ask him some questions. First, though, he unrolled the gun belt, took out the pistol, and made sure it was in working order. He cleaned it as well as he could with a rag, but that would have to do until he could get the right tools. The belt had cartridges on it, so after dry-firing it to make sure it would fire, he loaded the gun, put it back in the holster, and strapped the gun belt on. The rifle he propped up in a corner.

Feeling fully dressed for the first time since coming to town, he left the room.

"Back so soon?" Murphy asked, surprised. He was wiping his hands on a towel.

"I feel like my head's coming off, Doc," Lancaster said.

"Yeah, well, that'll happen when somebody kicks you there. Let me give you something."

He went into the other room, came back, and handed Lancaster an envelope.

"It's a powder, for the headache," the doctor said. "You dissolve it in a glass of water."

"Thanks, Doc."

"Wait."

The doctor went into the other room

71

again, came back with a glass of cloudy water.

"Here, drink this," he said. "I already put some in there."

Lancaster drank it and handed the glass back. "Thanks."

"Anything else I can do for you?"

"Well, yeah . . . can we talk a minute?"

"Sure. Whataya want to talk about?"

"My memory."

The doctor waved him to a chair and sat down himself at his desk.

"You said my memory might or might not come back," Lancaster said.

"That's true."

"So it's possible I could've seen the faces of the men who ambushed me, and I'll remember later?"

"It's possible," the doctor said. "Why? Are you seeing faces?"

"I'm seeing . . . flashes of things," Lancaster said. "You know . . . the boots . . . the desert . . . some figures . . . hearing voices, but never seeing faces. I need to see some faces."

"Mr. Lancaster, I think you should prepare yourself for the possibility that these memories may never fill in for you. They may never come back."

"But they've got to come back," Lancaster

said. "How the hell am I ever gonna find these guys if it doesn't come back?"

"You may not find them," the doctor said. "Or you may just have to use whatever information your memory is givin' you."

"Boots," Lancaster said.

"What kind of boots?" the doctor asked. "What color? What style? What kind of stitching? How many? You can learn a lot from a man about his boots."

"I guess . . ."

"I also suggest you don't push it," the doctor said. "If the memories are gonna come back, let them come back on their own."

Lancaster rubbed his head.

"Better yet?"

"Yeah," he said, "yeah, it's letting up. I think I'll go get some breakfast." He stood up. "Thanks, Doc. What do I owe you?"

"Nothin'," the doctor said. "Part of the service."

"Thanks, again," Lancaster said, and left.

SIXTEEN

Lancaster finally decided he had time for a leisurely breakfast, but he spent the whole time still trying to plug the holes in his memory.

He thought about what the doctor had said. What kind of boots? He'd never paid much attention to men's boots before — unless they were heels up on the ground. What could a man's boots tell you about him?

He thought back to being kicked, staring off into space, trying to bring it into focus. What he remembered mostly were toes and heels. Heels. That meant he was not only kicked, but stomped. But still, they made no attempt to kill him, only to hurt him. And they could have done worse than that. They could have maimed him. What did that mean? That they wanted to make it difficult for him to survive, but not impossible?

They wanted him to die in the desert, but

not without a fighting chance?

But he was thinking about this the wrong way.

It wasn't the three men who were making the decisions. He recalled a scrap of conversation that made him believe that they had been hired by somebody, and they must have had specific instructions.

So who wanted him dead?

The list was too damn long.

In his days as a gun for hire, he'd killed a lot of people — people he didn't know, people he was hired to kill. He always did it from the front, though, never from behind, never an ambush. Anybody he killed always had a fair chance to kill him first.

But family members probably wouldn't appreciate the distinction. There might be somebody out there who hated him enough to hire somebody to leave him alone in the desert to die.

It would be impossible for him to figure out who it was, though. There were just too many. And who knew how many he'd forgotten during the few years he'd been a drunk?

And now, getting kicked in the head hadn't done his memory much good, either.

He'd gone to the doctor to talk, for either solace or advice. Maybe what he should do was take the doctor's advice, and let the memories come back on their own.

Meanwhile, there was the horse to consider. And he still had to come up with a way to make some money.

From breakfast he went right to the livery to see Mal.

"Mornin', Lancaster."

"Mal." They shook hands. "How's he's going?"

"Crow Bait?" Mal asked. "He's already surprised me."

"How?"

"The way he eats," Mal said. "Horse eats like an animal twice his size."

"Yeah? That's good, right?"

"It's good if he puts on weight," Mal said. "If he eats like that and he don't put on weight, then I don't know what to tell you."

"Well, like I said yesterday," Lancaster replied, "I guess we'll just have to wait and see."

"You wanna take a look at him?"

"Sure, why not?"

"Go on back."

"Thanks."

"How's that gun feel?"

Lancaster stopped and looked down at the gun on his hip.

"It feels good," he said. "I just need to clean it a little better."

"I've got a kit for that," Mal said. "I'll give it to you before you leave."

"I'll pay you —"

Mal waved away any mention of payment.

"Just bring it back when you return everything else," he said.

"Okay."

Lancaster walked to the stall where Crow Bait stood, head in. The horse's rear end was probably the only part of it that looked normal. Maybe that big rump was where his stamina came from.

Lancaster patted the rump, walked farther into the stall, and held the horse's head, patted his nose.

"How you doin', boy?" he asked. "Man, you are ugly but you saved my life, so to me you're the most beautiful horse alive."

Crow Bait nodded his head and poked at Lancaster's hand.

"You want a treat? I got nothing for you, but I'll make sure I do from now on."

"Here," he heard from behind him. He turned and Mal was holding out a couple of green apples. "He likes 'em."

"They sour?"

"Yeah," Mal said. "I found out he doesn't like sweet."

77

Sweet?
Suddenly, it went dark.

78

SEVENTEEN

"What happened?"

Lancaster was looking up at Mal's face.

"You blacked out," Mal said. "I caught you when you fell."

"Fell?"

Lancaster pushed himself to a seated position and looked around. He was still in the livery, just outside Crow Bait's stall.

"Maybe you shouldn't get up yet," Mal said.

"Give me a hand," Lancaster said.

"Okay."

Mal pulled Lancaster to his feet. There was a brief moment of dizziness, and then he stood solid.

"You all right?"

"Yeah, yeah," Lancaster said. "I don't know what happened."

"You just ain't recovered from bein' kicked in the head," Mal said. "Gonna take a while."

79

"Yeah, you're probably right."

"Maybe you should go back to the doc."

"I've been to see him a few times already," Lancaster said. "He says I should recover. What I'm worried about is my memory. If that doesn't come back, then I won't be able to track down the three men who bushwhacked me, and find out who hired them."

"You think somebody hired them to do it?"

"That's about the only thing I'm sure of," Lancaster said.

"How can you be that sure?"

"I heard them talking. I didn't hear everything, but one of them said that killing me wasn't what they were supposed to do, or something like that. I'm sure they were hired."

"Men like you and me," Mal said, "we have a lot of people in our past who'd like to see us dead."

"I know it."

"You had a funny look on your face just before you fell," Mal said. "You sure —"

"Wait a minute," Lancaster said. "I remember . . . you said something just before . . . what was it?"

"We were talking about the apples," Mal said. "You mean the apples?"

"Something about apples . . ."

"I said Crow Bait liked the sour ones, not the sweet ones."

Sweet.

"That was it," Lancaster said.

"What?"

"Sweet."

"What about it?"

"Wait," Lancaster said, "give me a minute."

He went back into his patchy memory with the word *sweet,* trying to find a lace where it would fit . . . and there it was. . . .

"I've got it!" he said. "Just before I got kicked in the head the last time, somebody said, 'Sweet, don't.' "

"So one of them was named Sweet," Mal said. "Well, that's a helluva lot more than you had before. You ever know a man named Sweet?"

"No," Lancaster said, "but I'm going to."

Lancaster went from the livery to the sheriff's office, to see if the lawman knew anyone in the area named Sweet.

"Sweet?" the lawman asked. "That's all you've got? No first name?"

"For all I know, that is his first name," Lancaster said.

Sheriff Race sat back in his chair, took off his hat, and scratched his balding head.

"The name doesn't sound familiar to me," he said, replacing his hat. "I'll take a look through some of the posters I have, though."

"I'd be obliged, Sheriff," Lancaster said.

"So your memory's startin' to come back?" Race asked.

"Not completely," Lancaster said. "In fact, that's all I have right now."

"Well, a name is at least somethin' to go on," Race said. "I find anything in my paper and I'll let you know."

"Thanks, Sheriff."

Lancaster left the sheriff's office and walked over to the Wells Fargo office. He found Andy Black seated behind his desk.

"Lancaster," Andy said, "I was just wonderin' about you."

"Thought I'd check in with you, seeing as how you staked me," Lancaster said.

"Have a seat. Coffee?"

Lancaster sat and said, "No, thanks. I actually came in to ask you a question."

"Ask," Andy said, sitting back in his chair.

"You ever heard of a man named Sweet?"

"I knew Hal Sweet, worked for Wells Fargo in San Francisco years ago. But he's dead."

"Nobody around here?"

Andy knitted those bushy brows. "Not that I can think of. Unless he's come around lately and I just don't know 'im."

"Okay, then," Lancaster said, preparing to stand.

"What's this about?"

Lancaster took a few moments to explain to Andy how he recalled the name.

"Sounds like a breakthrough."

"A small one," Lancaster said. "Nothing else came through with it."

"Well, this is a good sign, though," Andy said. "Just give it some time."

"That's what I'm doing, Andy," Lancaster said. "There ain't much else to do."

EIGHTEEN

"Beer," he said to the bartender.

"Cold, right?" the bartender asked with a grin.

Lancaster was back in the K.O. Saloon again, having a cold beer, but what he really wanted was to talk with the bartender.

"Exactly."

"Comin' up."

The barman brought the beer, with a nice head on it, and asked, "Stayin' in town a while?"

"Just long enough for my horse to heal," Lancaster said. He didn't bother to mention that he also had some healing to do.

"What's your name?" the barman asked.

"Lancaster."

"Mine's Lucky."

"Lucky?"

The man grinned, showing some gaps in his teeth. "I was pretty lucky my first five or six fights in the ring."

"Then what happened?" Lancaster asked.

Lucky shrugged.

"Then I ran outta luck and ran into a guy who could fight," he said. "I quit after that. Didn't wanna get my brains bashed in."

"Sounds like it was a good decision. This place yours?"

"It is. Well, at least I'll know what you want when you come in now," Lucky said, and moved on to another customer.

Lancaster nursed his beer and once again tried to force his memories to come together. When that didn't work he started thinking about a man called Sweet. Andy was right. If Sweet had come to town with his cronies before, or after, the ambush, chances were nobody would know any of them.

Except maybe for one person.

Lancaster waved the bartender back over.

"Another one?"

"No, thanks," Lancaster said. "Have you seen Sweet around lately?"

"Sweet?" The bartender looked confused.

"A man named Sweet."

"First name? Last name?"

"Just Sweet."

The man shook his head. "I don't know him."

"Never heard the name?"

The bartender gave it a thought, then shook his head and said, "No. Is he supposed to be from town?"

"I don't know," Lancaster said. "It's more likely he was a stranger in town, had two other men with him."

"Three strangers, one named Sweet," the bartender repeated. "What do they look like?"

"Trail clothes," Lancaster said, "thirties or forties, might've looked like they just rode in off the desert." He was guessing at the ages.

"We get lots of men in here who rode in off the desert," the bartender said. "But I don't remember three together in the past week or so. That help?"

"Actually, it does," Lancaster said. "Thanks."

"Other saloons in town," the bartender said. "You might wanna check with the bartenders there. Maybe your guys just never came in here."

"That's good thinking," Lancaster said. "Thanks."

He turned and looked around the saloon. It was still too early for business to pick up, and there were only a few men in the place. The other saloons in town would probably be the same. He left his unfinished beer on the bar, figuring he'd have to drink at least half of one in each saloon, trying to find a bartender who knew a man named Sweet.

Three saloons later Lancaster still didn't know any more about Sweet than he did before, and he was starting to feel the effects of the beer. He knew he had to stop now, or he'd end up switching to whiskey, and then all the hard work he'd done crawling out of the bottle would be for nothing. He'd be a drunk again. It didn't take much to go back down that road.

He had to accept the fact that Sweet — whoever he was — had either not come to Laughlin or had laid very low when he was there.

Lancaster had a name. And he had a horse — and himself — to nurse back to health. He hoped the rest of it would come to him.

It was early to turn in, but these weren't normal circumstances. He needed the rest, and he needed to sleep off the beer. A short nap, and then a meal, should fix him up.

NINETEEN

Twenty miles outside Kingman, Arizona

The three men reined in, looked at the three signs on the signpost. One of them said HENDERSON, NV. 77 MILES, pointing north.

"That's where I'm headed," Adderly said. He looked at the other two men. "You comin'?"

Sweet shook his head. "I'm gettin' away from here, not goin' back into Nevada."

The third man, Cardiff, laughed and said, "You really think Lancaster walked outta that desert?"

"I ain't takin' any chances," Sweet said. "I'm headin' for Flagstaff."

Adderly looked at Cardiff. "Where ya goin'?"

"I got a girl in Peach Springs."

Adderly looked at the signpost. There was nothing there for Peach Springs.

"Where the hell is that?" he asked.

88

"About forty miles northeast," Cardiff said. He looked at Sweet. "I'll ride a short way with you."

"Fine with me."

Sweet looked at Adderly. "You're crazy to go back into Nevada."

"Listen," he said, "as long as we stay away from Laughlin and Desert Hills, we should be okay."

"Suit yourself," Sweet said. He looked at Cardiff. "You ready?"

"Ready."

"See you fellas somewhere down the trail," Adderly said.

As he rode off, Sweet said to Cardiff, "I don't wanna work with him again."

"No, me neither," Cardiff said.

"You hear him say my name when we had Lancaster down?" Sweet asked.

"Is that what's botherin' you?" Cardiff asked. "I just don't like the way he smells."

"He said my name," Sweet said. "What if Lancaster does walk out of that desert?"

"Then I guess he'll be lookin' for you," Cardiff said.

"That's why I'm headin' for Flagstaff."

And that's why, Cardiff thought, I'm only ridin' a short way with you.

TWENTY

Lancaster woke refreshed and ready for a steak. There was a small dining room in the hotel, but he decided to go out and find out if Laughlin had a good steak house.

As he hit the street, dusk was nudging its way in. He'd slept for almost an hour, and while he still had aches and pains and a slight headache, he felt better than he had in days.

He started walking, keeping an eye out for a likely café or restaurant, when suddenly a man appeared in front of him. Actually, he didn't just appear, he stepped out from an alley. Lancaster put his hand on his gun and eyed the man warily.

"You Lancaster?"

"Who wants to know?"

The man was in his thirties, thin and trembling, had black stubble on his face that gleamed with sweat. He licked his lips, then wiped them with the back of his hand. He was not wearing a gun.

"I heard you were lookin' fer a man called Sweet?" the man said.

"Are you Sweet?"

"N-no, naw, not me," the man said. "B-but I kn-know him."

"Where is he?"

"Um, wh-what's it worth to ya?"

"I don't have any money."

The man frowned, looked like he was about to cry. "N-nothin'?"

"No."

"Wh-what about a drink?" the man asked. "One drink?"

"Look, friend," Lancaster said, "Sweet and his two friends almost killed me, left me stranded in the desert to die. That's why I'm looking for them. Now, what do you think I'm gonna do when I find him?"

"Um, k-kill 'im?"

"So what do you think I'll do to you for the information?"

"Jeez, mister, I'm j-just tryin' ta get a drink," the drunk said.

"Is this information good?" Lancaster asked. "Because if you're lyin' to me —"

"I — I ain't lyin', mister," the man said. "Ask anybody, Bud Stall don't lie. I'm a drunk, but I ain't a liar."

"Okay," Lancaster said, "okay, Stall, come

91

with me."

They walked into the saloon and were ignored as they walked to the bar. Lancaster found a space, used his elbows to make it big enough for two. The men on either side misinterpreted and thought that Stall had been elbowing them.

"Goddamnit, Bud!" one of them said. "You elbow me again I'm gonna stomp you into a mud puddle."

The speaker was shorter than Stall, but much bulkier. He was, however, shorter than Lancaster, who stared down at him.

"That was me, friend," he said. "You want to try stomping me into a mud puddle?"

The man eyed Lancaster and backed off.

"Hey, friend, no harm," he said. "I just thought this drunk was pushin' me."

"This drunk happens to be a friend of mine and I'm buying him a drink. Got a problem with that?"

"Nossir," the man said. "No problem. In fact, I — I'll give ya some more space."

The man then walked quickly to the batwing doors and out.

"Step up, Bud," Lancaster said.

"Thank you, Mr. Lancaster."

Lucky came along and asked, "He with you, Lancaster?"

"He is, Lucky. Give him a drink."

"Whiskey," Stall said.

"Beer for you?" Lucky asked.

"No, nothing for me."

"Whiskey," Lucky said. He got a shot glass and a bottle and filled it.

Stall reached for the glass, but Lancaster stopped him.

"The information first, Stall," he said, "then the drink."

Stall licked his lips and stared at the drink. Again, he looked like he was going to cry.

"S-Sweet came to town with two other men a few days ago," he said. "Th-they drank at a small saloon on the edge of town, stayed in a run-down hotel there, and then left before you got to town."

So they had come to town after leaving him in the desert.

"How many days ago did they leave?"

" 'Bout five, I guess."

"Do you know where they went?"

"I — I was drinkin' in the saloon when they was there," Stall said. "Heard one of them say something about Henderson."

"Henderson?"

"Town some north of here," Stall said.

"Was it Sweet?" Lancaster asked. "Did he say he was going to Henderson?"

"I was pretty drunk," Stall said, "but I don't think it was him."

"What were the names of the other two men?"

"I dunno," Stall said, "but you could get that from the hotel they stayed in, or from the bartender in that saloon. He s-seemed to know them."

"What's the name of the saloon?"

"Ain't got a name."

"What about the hotel?"

"D-down the street from the saloon. Called the Autry House Hotel."

"That it?" Lancaster asked. "That all you got?"

"That's all I can remember now, but a drink might help," Stall said.

Lancaster removed his hand from Stall's arm and said, "Go ahead."

Stall's hand was trembling, but he managed to get the glass to his lips without spilling a drop. There was a noticeable lessening to the tremble as he set the glass down and breathed a sigh of relief.

TWENTY-ONE

Lancaster bought Stall one more drink before sending him on his way.

"You think of anything else, you let me know," he warned Stall.

"Yessir, I'll do 'er."

Stall left the saloon and Lucky waved Lancaster over.

"Why are you buyin' drinks for the town drunk?" he asked.

"He said he had information about Sweet," Lancaster said.

"And you believed him?"

"He's a drunk, but is he a liar?"

"Well, no, not usually," Lucky answered.

"You think he'd lie for a drink?"

"Well, he's a drunk."

"He was telling me about some saloon at the edge of town with no name, and a hotel called the Autry."

"Both cater to lowlifes and cheats, probably killers. So, yeah, if your guy was in

95

town he was probably there."

"Well, I guess I'll go and have a look."

"Be careful," Lucky said. "I wouldn't go there without somebody to watch your back. That's the north end of town, a pretty dangerous area."

Lancaster considered asking Lucky if he'd go with him, but decided against it. The man had a business to run, and no reason to take a hand in Lancaster's game.

"Much obliged, Lucky."

"Sure."

"Hey," Lancaster said, before leaving, "where can I get a good steak?"

"Got just the place for ya. . . ."

Lucky directed Lancaster to a place called Rachel's Café. "Rachel's ugly as sin, but man, she can cook," he said.

Lancaster entered and found the place with about half of its dozen tables taken. A young girl was waiting tables, and was much too pretty — and too young — to be Rachel. As she approached him with a weary smile, he noticed that at one table Mal was sitting alone, working on a steak. As she reached him Mal saw him and waved him over.

"I'm joining him," he said, pointing. "And I'll have a steak dinner."

"Yessir. Comin' up."

Lancaster walked to Mal's table and sat down.

"How'd you find this place?" Mal asked.

"The bartender at the K.O. told me about it," Lancaster said.

"I gotta tell Lucky to keep his mouth shut," Mal said. "Don't want everybody findin' this place."

There was a pitcher of beer and a pitcher of water on the table. In front of Lancaster was a glass, sitting upside down. He righted it and filled it with water.

"No beer?" Mal asked.

"I hit my limit today," Lancaster said.

While he waited for his meal, he told Mal how he had managed to do that, and also told him about his conversation with Bud Stall.

"Well, Stall was right. He may be a drunk, but he's not usually a liar."

"I heard that."

The girl brought him his dinner, which was a steak that practically took up the entire plate, with some vegetables around it.

"So what are you gonna do?" Mal asked.

"I'm going to the north end of town to see what I can find out at that saloon, and that hotel."

"That's not an area to go to without

somebody to watch your back," Mal said.

"That's what I've heard."

"I wish I could offer to go with ya," Mal said, "but for one thing, that's my gun you're wearin' . . ."

"I understand."

"And for another, I just don't wear a gun anymore," Mal finished.

"I said I understand, Mal."

"But I think I know somebody who'll go with ya," Mal said.

"I can go alone," Lancaster said.

"Normally, I wouldn't question that, Lancaster, but I was around to catch you when you fell, remember?"

"I remember," Lancaster said around a hunk of steak and onions.

"So I think you need somebody to watch your back."

"Who do you have in mind?"

"A friend of mine," Mal said. "After we finish here I'll take you over to meet him."

"Is he a good hand with a gun?" Lancaster asked.

"A gun, a knife, pretty much any weapon," Mal said. "You'll see."

Twenty-Two

After they finished eating, Mal took Lancaster about as far from the dangerous north end as you could get, the southern end of town.

"This looks deserted," Lancaster said as he looked at the buildings.

"It mostly is," Mal said.

"And this is where your friend lives?"

"This is where he prefers to live, yeah," Mal said. "He doesn't like a lot of people."

"But he likes you?"

"Maybe," Mal said, "he dislikes me a little less than he does most people."

"I think I can understand feelings like that," Lancaster said.

"It's over here."

Mal led Lancaster to one of the abandoned-looking buildings. They approached the door and before Mal knocked he said, "Stand to the side. He's been known to fire a shot through the door at the

99

sound of a knock."

"Thanks for the warning."

Mal knocked, waited, then knocked again.

"Mal, that you?" a voice called.

"How'd you know?"

"Nobody else has the nerve to knock on my door," the voice said. "You alone?"

"No, I brought a friend."

"I got no friends."

"Come on, Ledge," Mal shouted. "Open up!"

A few moments went by and then Lancaster heard the lock turn and the door opened.

"Come on in," the voice said.

"Ledge?" Lancaster asked.

"His name's Ledger," Mal said. "Ben Ledger, but he goes by Ledge."

Lancaster shrugged. After all, he and Mal had not exchanged anything but single names.

They entered and Lancaster was surprised. While the building looked like no more than a run-down cabin on the outside, the inside looked and smelled brand-new. He felt as if he was standing in a new house, with solid walls, wooden floors, a new fireplace, and a modern-looking kitchen with a water pump to bring water inside.

"Impressive," he said.

"Thanks," Ledge said. "Did all the work

myself."

Lancaster turned to face him. Again, he was surprised. Ledge was tall, powerfully built, with a head of shoulder-length snow-white hair. His face was heavily lined, as was his neck. His eyes, though, were clear and sky blue. His face looked sixty, but his body, his stance, his eyes, all bespoke a man much younger.

"Ledge, this is Lancaster," Mal said.

"Lancaster?" the tall man asked. "I know that name."

Lancaster didn't say anything.

"You got a taste?" Mal asked.

"Don't I always?" Ledge asked.

He grabbed a jug from a table, pulled out the cork, and passed it over. Mal accepted it and took a swig. He turned to Lancaster, who shook his head.

"Just a taste," Mal said. "To be polite."

Lancaster took the jug, took a small taste, just enough to wet his lips. The stuff had a kick like a mule, and he was just able to keep himself from choking. He handed the jug back to Ledge.

"Money gun, right?" Ledge asked.

"I was," Lancaster said. "That was a while ago."

"Quit?"

Lancaster nodded.

"Gives him somethin' in common with you, don't it, Mal?" Ledge asked.

"Yep."

Ledge looked at Lancaster's hip. "And that's your gun, ain't it?"

"Yep," Mal said again.

Ledge took a hefty swig from the jug and then put the cork back. "I guess somebody should tell me what's goin' on."

"It's like this . . ." Mal said, and went on to tell Ledge what had happened to Lancaster, and what he was trying to accomplish.

When he was finished, Ledge pulled the cork and took another heavy drink.

"Goddamn, but I hate bushwhackers," he said with feeling.

"Sounds like you have some experience," Lancaster said.

Ledge looked at Mal.

"Show him," Mal said.

Ledge turned around and lifted his shirt up to his shoulder blades. Three healed bullet holes, one above the other, alongside his spine.

"Each one missed my spine, or I'd be crippled, or dead." He dropped his shirt.

"He should be dead," Mal said. "Don't know how he pulled through."

"Stubborn," Ledge said, turning back

102

around. "I hate back-shooters and ambushers."

"And the men who shot you?"

"I tracked 'em and killed 'em," Ledge said. "Two of 'em. And now I'm gonna help you do the same. Just let me get outfitted."

There was another room, and Ledge quickly disappeared into it.

"I only need him to back me tonight," Lancaster said to Mal.

"He'll probably want to go all the way with you," Mal said. "He hates bushwhackers that much. But that'll be between you and him. Accept his help tonight, and deal with the rest when the time comes."

"Sounds like good advice."

Ledge reappeared, wearing a gun belt that held a pistol and a bowie knife. Across his chest was a bandolier that held extra cartridges and what looked like three throwing knives.

"You ready?" he asked.

TWENTY-THREE

Mal went back to his livery stables while Lancaster and Ledge walked clear across town, stopping first at the little saloon with no name.

"I been here before," Ledge said. "Usually a bunch of cutthroats."

"It's my play, so I'll do the talking," Lancaster said.

"Hey," Ledge said, "I'm just here to back you — but I gotta warn you . . ."

"About what?"

"When they see me they're gonna be curious."

"Good," Lancaster said. "Let 'em."

Lancaster walked through the batwing doors with Ledge close behind him. They walked directly to the bar, which was made of pitted, old wood. They were probably used to the bar getting destroyed in here, and easily replaced.

The place was small and doing a good

business. Most of the tables were taken and there was only a space or two left at the bar. Lancaster used his elbows again, as he had at the K.O., and when the other patrons saw Ledge with him, they willingly moved.

As Ledge had predicted, he and Lancaster were the center of attention. It was just not often that Ledge was seen in this part of town, let alone this saloon.

"Ledge," the bartender said. "Surprised to see you here. What can I getcha?" He was fat, with mean little eyes buried in fat pouches. He had only a few hairs on his head, yet he appeared to only be in his thirties.

"That's up to my friend here," Ledge said.

The bartender looked at Lancaster curiously. He wasn't used to having Ledge refer to someone as his friend.

"You remember a man named Sweet?" Lancaster asked. "Was in here last week with two other men."

The bartender stared at Lancaster, then looked at Ledge. "What's goin' on, Ledge?"

"If I was you, I'd answer the man's question."

"We don't like nobody comin' in here askin' no questions," the bartender said. "You oughtta know that, Ledge. And why you come in here wearin' a gun?"

105

"Because I'm thinkin' I might have to shoot somebody," Ledge replied.

"Sweet," Lancaster said again. "With two other men, all stayin' at the Autry House."

The bartender's eyes danced around in his head. He was either looking for help or just nervous that everyone in the room was now watching him to see what he'd say.

"Sweet, you say?"

"That's right."

"Wh-what's he look like?"

"Trail clothes, probably thirties. The three of them were probably alike."

"We gets lots of men —"

"Came in off the desert," Lancaster said. "Stayed a couple of days, maybe."

"I dunno —"

"Maybe you even sent them over to the Autry," Ledge said. "You been known to do that, right, Eddie?"

Eddie the bartender gave Ledge an exasperated look, as if to say, *Thanks a lot!* "Well, sometimes —"

"Think hard, Eddie," Ledge said. "Think real hard before you answer."

Eddie was being watched by everyone in the bar, but he was wilting beneath the twin stares of both Lancaster and Ledge.

"Sweet," he said, licking his lips. "Yeah, I think I remember somebody by that name.

I mighta sent them to the Autry — him and his friends, I mean."

"Did you ever hear them talking about where they might go after they left here?"

"I don't think —"

"I already heard from somebody who said he did hear them talking in here," Lancaster said, "so I'm just checking to see if you have the same information — or if you're going to lie."

Again, the bartender licked his lips. "Well . . . somebody mighta said somethin' about going to Henderson."

"Would it have been Sweet?"

"Now, that I really can't tell ya," Eddie said. "I don't rightly remember which one said it. And that's the truth."

Lancaster turned and looked at the room. Half of the eyes slid away, but the others stared boldly back at him, as if daring him to challenge them.

Lancaster was in the mood for a challenge.

"Anybody here remember a man named Sweet?" he asked. "With a couple of partners?"

"Why'n't ya go back where ya came from?" somebody asked. "Ya don't belong here, askin' questions."

Lancaster pushed away from the bar and stood straight up. Ledge followed his lead.

"Who said that?"

Nobody answered.

"Come on," Lancaster said, "you were brave enough to say something, be brave enough to take the credit."

No answer. More eyes slid away; just a few were brave enough to at least keep staring.

"Bunch of cowards," Lancaster said. "Now I see why you stay at this end of town and drink with the other yellow bellies."

He turned back to the bartender.

"I find out you lied to me, I'll be back to take this place apart," he said, "and I'm in just the mood to do it."

"Hey, I answered yer questions," Eddie said. "Why take it out on me?"

"Because I don't like the quality of your customers," Lancaster said.

Eddie cast an accusing glance at his customers. For a moment Lancaster thought the bartender would point out the speaker, but it didn't happen.

Lancaster looked at Ledge. "You got any idea who spoke?"

"I got a couple," Ledge said. "I just might have a couple."

TWENTY-FOUR

Ledge left the bar and walked over to a table of three men. Two of them looked away, but one of them held Ledge's stare.

"What about you, Jimmy? You the big mouth?" Ledge asked.

Still staring back, the man named Jimmy said, "If it was me, Ledge, I'd say so."

Ledge looked over at Lancaster. "Yeah, he's right. He would."

Ledge moved on to another table, this one with two men. He put his hand on the shoulder of a man who jumped at the touch.

"This is Nappy, though. He'd speak up from out of a crowd, where it was safe, and then hide. Wouldn't you, Nappy?"

"Whataya pickin' on me fer, Ledge?" Nappy asked. "I din't do nothin' to you."

"I think you got a big mouth, Nappy," Ledge said. "What do you know about Sweet and his friends?"

"Nothin'."

Lancaster saw Ledge's hand close on Nappy's shoulder. There was a lot of strength in that hand, and it was being brought to bear on the smaller man, who winced and wilted under the pressure.

"Okay, okay," he whined. "I had a drink with Sweet and his friends."

"What were his friends' names?" Lancaster asked.

"I dunno," Nappy said. "I only talked ta Sweet. The other two just listened."

"What'd you talk about?"

"This and that."

Ledge's hand closed again.

"Ow!" Nappy looked around for help, but there was none available. "Okay. We talked about the desert, and how not many men come walkin' in off it."

"Why was Sweet talking about that?" Ledge asked.

"He just seemed interested in hearin' if anybody had ever made it on foot," Nappy said. "Like he was nervous about it or somethin'."

Why would Sweet be nervous about leaving Lancaster in the desert — unless he was afraid that Lancaster would successfully walk out?

Maybe he remembered — as Lancaster had — that one of the other men had said his name.

Ledge looked over at Lancaster, who nodded. The big man took his hand off Nappy's shoulder and walked back to stand by Lancaster at the bar.

"Anybody else got anything to say?" Lancaster demanded.

There was no response. He looked at Eddie the bartender again. "Remember what I said."

"I ain't lyin' about nothin'," Eddie said, spreading his hands helplessly.

"Let's go," Lancaster said to Ledge.

"You first," Ledge said.

Lancaster left, Ledge covering his back, and then the big man backed out, as well.

Outside the saloon Ledge asked, "Did you get what you wanted?"

"I think so," Lancaster said, "but maybe we can get more at the Autry."

"Let's go, then," Ledge said, "before Eddie sends somebody over there to warn them we're comin'."

TWENTY-FIVE

The Autry was a run-down two-story hotel
that looked one good storm away from being a pile of rubble.

"You know the owner here?" Lancaster
asked.

"No," Ledge said. "I knew the previous
owner, but he was killed."

"By the present owner?"

"No, by a former guest."

"What about clerks?" Lancaster asked.
"Know any of the clerks?"

"That depends," Ledge said with a shrug.
"Why don't we just go in and see who's
working? I might know 'em, but I might
not."

They approached the hotel and entered
the lobby. There were the remnants of a
couple of chairs on the floor, as if there had
just been a fight. Behind the desk a bored
clerk watched them as they came up to the
desk.

112

"You ain't lookin' fer a room," he said.

"How do you know?" Lancaster asked

"I can tell. You got somethin' on yer mind."

"I got some questions," Lancaster agreed. "Are you gonna have some answers?"

"I guess that depends on how bad you want answers," the clerk said. He was young and cocky for a young fellow who worked in a dump.

"How bad do I need to?" Lancaster asked.

"Well, you can threaten me, maybe beat me up," the clerk said, "but that'll take longer."

"Longer than what?"

"Payin' me."

The young man seemed pretty sure of himself. Lancaster noticed he had one hand in view and the other below the desk. What were the chances he had a gun underneath the desk?

"Well," Lancaster said, "I could pay you, but the fact of the matter is I don't have any money, so we're gonna have to go another way."

"Hey, I gotta gu—"

Working as one, Lancaster and Ledge picked up the front desk and rammed it and the clerk against the wall behind them. The clerk cried out, both hands going out to try

113

to protect himself.

Lancaster and Ledge pulled the flimsy desk away and tossed it aside, where it fell to pieces. On the floor at their feet was an old Navy Colt that the clerk had been holding.

"Okay," Lancaster said, grabbing the clerk by the front of the shirt and pulling him up, "we went another way."

"Take it easy," the clerk said. "I'm just tryin' to make a few extra dollars."

"How about no money, and no beatin' up?" Ledge asked. "We'll just ask some questions and you answer 'em."

"Okay, then," the clerk said. "That'll work."

"I want to see your register for the past couple of weeks," Lancaster said.

"Why didn't you just say so? It's on the floor, there. Um, with my broken desk."

Ledge looked down at his feet, saw the book, and picked it up. He passed it to Lancaster, who let go of the clerk and opened the book.

"Here we go," Lancaster said. "It was actually about a week ahead of me. Sweet, Adderly, and Cardiff."

"You remember them?" Ledge asked.

"Who wouldn't remember a man named Sweet?" the clerk asked. "He was touchy about it."

"You ever hear them talk about where they were goin' when they left here?" Lancaster asked.

"You sure there ain't a few dollars in this for me?" the clerk asked.

"I can wrap the rest of this desk around your neck," Ledge said.

"Hey, okay," the clerk said. "I heard somethin' about Henderson, and I think one of them said somethin' about Peach City, or somethin' like that."

"Peach City?" Lancaster asked.

Ledge just shrugged.

"Never heard of it," he said.

"That it?" Lancaster asked the clerk.

"Hey, mister," he said, "that's all I heard."

Lancaster looked at Ledge again and the man said, "I think that's all we're gonna get."

Lancaster pushed the register into the clerk's chest. The man grabbed it with both arms.

As Lancaster and Ledge headed for the door, the clerk called out, "What am I gonna tell my boss happened to the desk?"

Lancaster turned, waved at the floor, and said, "Blame it on whoever broke these chairs."

As they went out the door, they heard the

115

clerk mutter, "That's actually not a bad idea."

TWENTY-SIX

Lancaster invited Ledge to the K.O. Saloon for a drink, but Ledge declined.

"I stay out of the saloons in town," he said.

"Why's that?" Lancaster asked.

"I get into too much trouble when I go to saloons," Ledge said. "That's why I make my own squeezin's. I can get drunk at home without gettin' into any trouble."

"Makes sense."

"So come back and share a jug."

"I can't."

"Why?"

"Isn't so long ago I was a drunk, Ledge," Lancaster said. "I can't risk it again."

"I understand," Ledge said. "I can make a pot of coffee, and then we can talk about what we're gonna do next."

"What we're gonna do?"

"Yeah," Ledge said, "to track those bastards who bushwhacked you."

They were walking back to Ledge's place.

"Ledge, I don't expect you to pick up and leave your home to help me track them down."

"You gonna track three men alone?"

"I'm gonna track 'em one at a time."

"Well," Ledge said, "what the hell, let's have some coffee and talk about it. Maybe I can say somethin' that'll help."

"What kind of horse?" Ledge asked.

"Crow Bait."

"That's his name or what he is?"

"It's what he looked like when we found each other on the desert," Lancaster said, "but he walked me out of there. He saved my life."

"So you're gonna stay with him to track these bastards?"

"Ledge, it's amazing the stamina this horse had," Lancaster said. "With some feed in him and a few pounds on him, there's no telling how long he can go."

"You can get a better horse, ya know," Ledge said.

"That would cost money, and I'm kind of short right now," Lancaster said.

"Well, I can't help ya there," Ledge said. "I ain't got much money myself."

"That's okay," Lancaster said. "My friend over at Wells Fargo staked me enough to get outfitted. And Mal helped a lot."

"Then you're ready to go."

"Yeah, and don't take offense, but I'd just as soon do this alone," Lancaster said. "I'm kind of used to working that way."

"Hell, I ain't takin' offense," Ledge said. "This is your business. Believe me, I know how it feels. It took me eight months to track the two who shot me in the back, but I got 'em, and I felt great about it. Folks say revenge ain't worth it, but I'm here to tell you, it is."

"Well, I'm intent on mine, and nobody's gonna talk me out of it," Lancaster said.

"Well, now that you have a couple of places to check out, when will you be leavin'?"

"Soon," Lancaster said. "I probably need a couple more days myself, and Crow Bait can use the extra feed time. But I'm not gonna wait much longer than that. I don't want those jaspers getting too big a head start on me. I've already got a lot of time to make up."

"Slow and steady, Lancaster," Ledge said. "I'm here ta tell ya that slow and steady will do it."

"Well, I think I got the right horse for that," Lancaster said.

He did, as long as Crow Bait didn't suddenly revert to that condition. The animal did still look awful!

Lancaster finished his coffee with Ledge and thanked the man for backing his play. When he left Ledge's place he walked over to the livery and found Mal still awake and working.

"How'd it go?" he asked.

"Got what I needed," Lancaster said, "without firing a shot."

"That's good."

"Ledge was a big help. Thanks for that."

"He gonna track 'em with you?"

"He would, but I asked him not to."

"You wanna do this alone, huh?"

"That's right."

"Can't blame you."

"You ever heard of a place called Peach City?"

"No," Mal said, "but I heard of Peach Springs."

"Where's that?"

"It's a small town in Arizona, east of Henderson."

"That's gotta be it, then," Lancaster said. "Henderson and Peach Springs."

"And you're still takin' Crow Bait?"

"Unless you tell me he can't make it."

"Ain't gonna tell ya that," Mal said. "He

looks awful, but he seems to be okay."

"So he'll make it?"

"He should make it," Mal said, "if that's good enough for you."

"It's good enough for me."

TWENTY-SEVEN

Three days later Lancaster went to Doc Murphy's to get checked out, then went to Mal's livery to check on Crow Bait. Both of them got a clean bill of health, although Crow Bait still looked like hell.

Actually, so did Lancaster.

But it didn't matter how they looked. What mattered was how they felt.

"He's kickin' down the stall," Mal said. "I'm amazed. Based just on looks, you wouldn't look at him twice. But I think you're right about him. It's all about stamina."

"Is there any chance —" Lancaster said, then stopped himself.

"What?" Mal asked. "That he'll suddenly become the horse he looks like?"

Lancaster nodded.

"Well, is there any chance you'll suddenly become the man you look like?"

"Every day," Lancaster said.

"There ya go, then," Mal said. "You'll both be takin' a chance on each other."

When Lancaster got back to his hotel, there was a message for him with the clerk. It was from Andy Black, asking if he'd come over and see him as soon as he got the note.

He did.

Andy looked up as Lancaster entered and stood up.

"Thanks for comin' over so fast, Lancaster."

"I didn't know when you left the note."

"It was only about an hour ago. Have a seat. Somethin' to drink? Coffee?"

"Coffee's good."

Andy poured two cups of coffee, passed one over to Lancaster, then sat behind his desk.

"What's goin' on, Andy?"

"How'd you like to make some money?"

"What kind of money?"

"Good money."

"I don't do that kind of work anymore, Andy," Lancaster said.

"No, not that," Andy said. "Wells Fargo needs somebody tracked down and brought in."

"Bounty hunter?"

123

"If you're workin' for us," Andy said, "it ain't called that."

Andy had a point. And Lancaster did need to put some money together.

"How much are we talkin' about?"

"A lot," Andy said. "Enough for you to get properly outfitted and buy a new horse."

"I've got a horse."

"Well, whatever you need, then."

"Who am I hunting, Andy?"

Andy sat back and took a moment. "It's Gerald Beck."

"Gerry Beck?"

Andy nodded.

"Five thousand dollars," he said. "A thousand in advance, four when you bring him in."

"Alive?"

"Just bring him in," Andy said. "He's been robbin' us blind for years, and it's time to stop it . . . for good."

Now it was Lancaster's turn to hesitate.

"What brought this on, Andy?" he asked. "Gerry's been at this for at least ten years."

"He robbed a Wells Fargo office earlier this week, killed two men — two clerks. Well, one clerk, and one agent."

"Like you?"

"Yes," Andy said, "exactly like me."

Lancaster had known Gerry Beck for

many years, although he hadn't seen him in about eight. There was a time when they rode together, worked together, but that went back even further. Over the past ten years, Beck had turned from hiring out his gun to robbing Wells Fargo stagecoaches, offices, and banks. Why, Lancaster didn't know, but he'd been making their lives hell for all that time and even the best Wells Fargo detectives — like Dodge and Hume — had been unable to bring him to justice.

But Lancaster had other things to do.

"You know what my plans are, Andy."

"Yeah, I do, Lancaster," he said. "That's why when I got the telegram from the main office I told them I'd get you."

"And why did you think I'd be interested?"

"Well, aside from the money," Andy said, "the office he hit was in Henderson."

TWENTY-EIGHT

When Lancaster rode into Henderson a week later, he had a thousand dollars in his pocket. Crow Bait had been steadfast the entire ride from Laughlin, had not faltered once. So far, so good with the animal.

Despite the fact that he'd been given a thousand dollars in advance by Wells Fargo, he decided to keep all of the borrowed outfit he'd gotten from Mal and use them to track down the bushwhackers. Mal's gun — though it had been in the trunk for a few years — had been well cared for and had served Mal well all through his life as a money gun. And Lancaster was committed to tracking these men down with the help of Crow Bait. When he was finished with both tasks, and he collected the rest of his fee, that was when he would outfit himself anew.

Actually, he had a thousand dollars minus what he had spent for some new clothes —

an extra shirt and an extra pair of jeans.

He was still wearing the same flat-brimmed black Stetson he always wore. At least they had left him that in the desert — which might have been an oversight. If you want a man to die in the desert, then take not only his horse and his water, but his hat.

Lancaster rode directly to the Wells Fargo office, tied Crow Bait off right outside, and walked in. There were two desks, one empty. Behind the other one sat a small man in his fifties, head down, working on some papers.

"Sam Worth?" Lancaster asked.

The man looked up. "I'm Worth. You Lancaster?"

"That's right."

"Come on in," Worth said. "Have a seat."

Lancaster pulled a chair over from the other desk and sat down.

Worth sat back, folding his arms. "So you're the man who's gonna bring in Gerald Beck when our best detectives haven't been able to do it?"

"That's me."

"What makes you think you can succeed where they couldn't?"

"I'm getting paid a lot of money to succeed," Lancaster said.

"That's it?"

"I happen to know Gerry Beck."

That surprised Worth. "You know him? How?"

"We rode together once."

"What are you, a reformed gunman?"

"Something like that," Lancaster said. "You want to tell me what happened?"

"Sure," Worth said. "Come on, I'll walk you through it. I was here by the safe, my partner was at his desk, and there was another man . . ."

After Worth finished laying out the way it happened, Lancaster said, "You got lucky."

"Whataya mean?"

"I mean all that flying lead and none hit you." Lancaster looked around. There were chunks taken out of the walls from the shooting. "You must have a guardian angel."

"What are you tryin' to say?" Worth asked.

"Nothing," Lancaster said. "I just know the way Gerry Beck works."

"And how's that?"

"He likes to get himself an edge."

"What kind of edge?" Worth went over and stood behind his desk. The fingers of his left hand were touching the handle of the top drawer.

"He likes to use an inside man when he can," Lancaster said. "He finds somebody

128

who needs money, or has a family."

Worth was easing the drawer open.

"Which one were you, Sam?" Lancaster asked. "And if you try to pull that gun out of the drawer, I'll kill you."

Worth pulled his hand away as if the drawer were hot.

"Now talk," Lancaster said. "Do you have family in town?"

"No."

"Then Gerry must have offered you money," Lancaster said. "A cut."

"H-he said he'd kill me if I didn't go along with him."

"If he was going to kill you, he would have done it when he was killing the other two," Lancaster said. "No, there was no threat. He was cutting you in. Did you get your money yet?"

Sam Worth licked his lips.

"No, you didn't get paid yet. So why are you still here?"

Worth frowned.

Lancaster laughed.

"You don't know where he is, do you?" he asked. "He pulled a fast one on you."

Sam Worth sank back in his chair with a defeated look on his face.

TWENTY-NINE

The sheriff came out of the cell blocks and hung the key on a wall hook. He turned and looked at Lancaster.

"I got a telegram that said you were coming," he said. "I didn't expect you to solve the robbery so soon after you got here."

"I got lucky, Sheriff Carver," Lancaster said. "I happened to know Gerry Beck's methods. And there was too much lead flying around that office for Worth not to have been hit. It had to be deliberate."

"Do you think he did any of the shootin'?" Carver asked.

"I don't know," Lancaster said. "He had a gun in his top drawer. You could check to see if it's been fired."

"You didn't do that?"

"Not part of my job," Lancaster said.

"But you questioned him."

"That was part of my job," he said.

"Did you find out anything?"

"Only that he was in on the job with Beck," Lancaster said.

"And you believe he doesn't know where Beck is?" Carver asked. "That they're not gonna meet and split the money?"

"No," Lancaster said. "I believe he was cheated by Beck, who left him here to take the rap."

Carver settled his bulk behind his desk. He was in his forties, had been sheriff of Henderson for over ten years. "So what are you gonna do now?"

"Try to find Beck."

"How?"

"I'll think about that over a steak," Lancaster said. "Where can I get a good one?"

"Across the street. Bessie's serves the best steak in town."

"Thanks."

Lancaster headed for the door, then stopped. "One other thing."

"What's that?"

"Have you ever heard of a man named Sweet?"

"Sweet? No."

"What about Adderly or Cardiff?"

Carver gave it some thought.

"I don't know those names, either," he said finally. "Why are you askin'?"

"I'm tracking them."

131

"All three?"

"That's right."

"Because of this job for Wells Fargo?"

"No," Lancaster said. "This is personal, and just happened to coincide with this job. I know that one of those three men came here in the past few weeks."

"Well, if they did they didn't have any contact with me," Carver said. "Looks like you better start checking hotel registers."

"And rooming houses," Lancaster said.

"So does this mean you'll be in town for a while?" the lawman asked.

"Overnight, at least," Lancaster said. "And I'll have to send a telegram back to Wells Fargo in Laughlin."

"Why's that?"

"To tell them they'll have to close down the local office until they can replace Sam Worth."

"They won't take too kindly to that," Carver said. "Bound to cost them some business."

"Unless they can replace him locally, which doesn't seem likely," Lancaster said, "they'll have no choice."

"Well, they only had the three men," Carver said. "Two are dead and now one's in my jail."

"I'm sure they'll be sending somebody

from the home office to handle everything," Lancaster said. "I'm going to go and get that steak now, and then I'll start checking around town."

"For those three men?"

"And for any trace of Gerry Beck," Lancaster said. "He must've spent some time with somebody, and knowing Gerry as I do, I'll probably have to start at the local whorehouse."

"Likes whores, does he?"

"He loves women, whores or not," Lancaster said, "and they like him."

"Well," Carver said, "even if Beck was in town long enough to go to the whorehouse, I didn't cross paths with him, either."

Lancaster didn't like the sound of that. Beck had to have been in town long enough to case the Wells Fargo office. And since he was working alone, he'd have taken his time. If the sheriff never came across either Beck or one of the other three, then he was the kind of lawman who ignored strangers in his town.

He was either a bad lawman or, after so many years at it in the same town, he'd become a lazy one.

THIRTY

The sheriff had been right about one thing. The steak at Bessie's was so good it must have been the best in town.

He'd stopped first at the livery to get Crow Bait taken care of. He'd gotten the expected reaction from the liveryman, paid the man to take good care of the horse, and left him scratching his head.

After finishing his steak and topping it off with a slice of pie, Lancaster started hitting the hotels and checking registers. He started with the hotel he was staying in, the Shamrock. They didn't show any guests named Sweet, Adderly, Cardiff, or Beck in the past month.

He'd arrived in town midday, so he had time to check the hotels and boardinghouses. It was dusk by the time he finished and he decided the saloons would be next, to see if any of the bartenders could help.

Henderson was a decent-sized town, with

more saloons than hotels. It took longer to get a bartender to give up information about one of his customers than the desk clerk at a hotel. Desk clerks could be bought cheaper.

In the saloons he had to order a beer, and drink at least half of it. He had to stop after four saloons, or end up drunk. The four bartenders he'd spoken to had never heard of any of the four men. Or so they claimed. He decided to leave the rest of the search for the morning.

He left the Hi-Lo Saloon and headed back to his hotel.

The bartender at the Hi-Lo took two beers to a table in the back. The two men stared up at him.

"We didn't order no beers," one of them said.

"Beck did," the bartender said.

"Beck?" the other asked.

"He told me if anybody was in askin' about him I should bring you some beers."

The bartender put them down.

"Who was askin'?"

"Tall guy with the flat-brimmed black hat who was just in here," the bartender said. "He's been askin' about four men."

"Four?"

"One of them is Beck."

"Who were the others?"

"Never heard of them."

"Was it us?" one of them asked.

The bartender looked at them and said, "I ain't never heard of you, either."

He walked away.

The two men looked at each other.

"Whataya think?" Bill Kent said.

"I think if this hadn't happened we'd be leavin' town tomorrow, and all we did was sit around and drink beer to earn our money," Wes Tyler said. "Now we gotta kill a guy."

"That's what Beck paid us for, Wes," Kent said. "Stay here one week, kill anybody who was lookin' for him."

"You know I'd rather earn my money sittin' around drinkin' beer, right?"

"I know it, but we can't do it."

"Why not?" Kent asked. "We can just pretend like we never heard what the bartender said."

"Beck will find out."

"We can blame the bartender."

"Beck will find out."

"Pretend like we left town without ever hearin' about it —"

"Beck will find —"

"I know, I know!" Kent said. "Beck will

136

find out and he'll kill us. I get it."

They sat there for a few moments in silence, and then Kent said, "Let's finish these fresh beers and then go get it done."

It took them a couple of hours to track down the man who'd been asking questions about Beck. They didn't mind that, because by now the fella would be in his bed, sound asleep.

"Always easier to kill a sleepin' man," Kent said to his partner.

"I know."

They were standing outside the hotel, getting themselves ready to go in.

"We're gonna have to kill the clerk, too," Kent said, "because he's gonna see us."

"Course he's gonna see us, because we have to ask him what room this Lancaster's in."

"Lancaster," Kent said. "Damn, but that name's familiar. I just can't place it."

"Never mind," Tyler said. "You can think about it later, after he's dead."

"Yeah, okay," Kent said. "Look, after the clerk gives us the room number, lemme kill 'im, okay? I hate hotel clerks. Snotty little bastards."

"Sure," Tyler said, "the clerk's yours. Are you ready to do this?"

"I'm ready," Kent said. "Let's go in."

They started in and Kent put his hand on Tyler's arm. "Wait, we gotta kill the bartender, too?"

"We'll talk about that later."

"Okay, but if we gotta kill the bartender, lemme do it," Kent begged. "I hate bartenders. Snotty little bastards!"

THIRTY-ONE

Kent and Tyler decided the best course of
action was the direct one. They'd kick in
the door of Lancaster's room and gun him
down while he was in bed. What could be
easier?

They crept down the hall, guns in their
hands, after leaving the clerk behind the
desk with a fatal knife wound in his chest.
They had flipped a coin to see who would
kick the door in. Tyler had won, so Kent
was upset, even though he'd gotten to kill
the clerk, like he wanted.

The floor creaked slightly beneath their
combined weight, but neither of them
noticed it. They were intent on what they
had to do.

They came to the door and positioned
themselves. Tyler was in front, Kent just
behind him, ready to fire. He could hardly
stand still, he enjoyed killing so much.

Tyler slammed his heel into the door just

beneath the doorknob. The door opened with a loud, splintering sound, but to the surprise of both men the first shot came from inside the room. . . .

Lancaster was ready for the two men. Because he knew Gerry Beck's methods, he figured the man had left one or two men behind to take care of anyone asking questions about him. It was the main reason he'd decided to retire to his room early. He hadn't expected them to take so long to find him, though, and had almost fallen asleep. When the floor creaked beneath their weight, he heard it, because he had noticed it when it creaked beneath him earlier in the day.

You had to notice things like that if you were going to survive as long as he had.

When he heard the creak, he sat up straight on the bed and palmed Mal's borrowed gun. He had spent some time earlier cleaning it, and dry-firing it to make sure it would function properly. He had supreme confidence in it as he waited for the door to open.

He was not, however, unmindful of the fact that someone might come through the window. He had perched the room's pitcher and basin there as an alarm system, and was

140

prepared for a double attack from both directions.

The door slammed open with a loud, splintering sound. A man with a gun was framed in the doorway and Lancaster fired once. He would have preferred a nonfatal wound, but didn't have the luxury of being that precise. He simply fired dead center and hoped for the best.

However, there was a second man behind the first, partially blocked from view, and suffering the same disadvantage.

Lancaster decided to get off the bed so as to present an off-center target.

Kent was shocked by the sound of the shot and the flash of the gun from inside the room, but not as shocked as Tyler, who took a bullet in the chest. He staggered back against Kent with a grunt, his gun falling from his hand.

Kent took a step back to let Tyler fall to the floor, and when he got a clear view of the room, he was looking at a man down on one knee, pointing a gun at him.

"Just twitch and you're dead," Lancaster said. "Be smart and drop it."

Kent had his gun in his hand and was tempted, but at that moment a memory clicked into place.

"Oh, damn," he said, "Lancaster," and dropped his gun.

THIRTY-TWO

"Inside," Lancaster said.

Kent moved into the room with his hands up.

"Close the door."

"Lancaster," Kent said, closing the door on his dead partner. "Now I remember. You used to ride with Beck."

"Long time ago," Lancaster said.

"I thought you were dead," Kent said. "I think even Beck thought you were dead, and now you're huntin' him?"

"That's right," Lancaster said. "And you're gonna tell me where he is."

"That's gonna be pretty hard," Kent said, "since I don't know where he is."

"Then he paid you in advance?"

"That's right."

"And you and your partner are just so honorable you did the job anyway, huh?"

"Don't kid yerself," Kent said. "If I thought I could've got away with it, I

143

woulda left town the day after he did."

"So you're afraid of him?"

"Damn right."

"Are you afraid of me?"

"Hell, no."

Lancaster cocked the hammer on his gun and said, "You should be."

"You were somethin' once, Lancaster," Kent said, "and you killed my partner, but you'll just kill me. What Beck will do to me . . ." He let it trail off.

Once Lancaster and Beck were alike. It seemed, over the years, that they had become very, very different. What was Beck like now that a man like this would rather die than face him?

"I tell you what," Lancaster said.

"You got an offer for me?"

"I do."

"Let's hear it."

"Let's you and me go lookin' for Beck."

"You crazy?" Kent asked. "After I screw up killin' ya, I'm gonna go with ya to find him? You know what he'd do to me?"

"No, but you keep asking me if I do, so I think I'd like to see."

"You're crazy," Kent said. "The law here won't let you take me."

"The law here's pretty lazy, or haven't you

144

noticed?" Lancaster asked. "What's your name?"

"Kent."

"Okay, Kent," Lancaster said. "Even if he is lazy, the sheriff should be here soon. Make up your mind. Tell me what you know about Beck, or come with me to find him."

"I told ya, I don't know nothin' —"

"You may not know, but you've got some idea where he went," Lancaster said. "Or where he'll be."

"You want me to guess?"

"If you give me your best guess, I'll leave you here when I go lookin' for him."

"You serious?"

"I am."

"And you'll believe me?"

"It ain't so much that I'll believe you," Lancaster said, "as it is I'll know if you're lying."

Kent looked as if he was giving the proposal some thought.

"I'd think in a hurry if I was you," Lancaster said. "You got until the sheriff gets here to make up your mind."

Kent looked at Lancaster and then said, "Okay, you got a deal."

145

THIRTY-THREE

When the sheriff showed up, Lancaster turned Kent over to him. The lawman collected some men and had the body of the dead Tyler carried out of the hotel.

"Looks like you'll need a new room," he said to Lancaster after the two men had been removed.

"Looks like."

"I wouldn't sleep too sound if I was you, though."

"Why? You know something I don't? Anybody else planning to kill me?"

"Not that I know of, but . . ."

"Don't worry, Sheriff," Lancaster said. "I'll try not to kill anyone else tonight."

"Yeah, well . . . I'd be much obliged. You leavin' tomorrow?"

"Yeah, but not too early. I got some of what I needed, but I hope to get the rest of it tomorrow."

"Let me know when you're ridin' out,"

146

Sheriff Carver said. "Then I can let out the breath that I'll be holdin'."

"I'll do that. I better go down and get another room from the clerk."

"Just grab any key," the sheriff said. "They killed the clerk."

"Sorry to hear it."

They walked down to the lobby together.

Lancaster woke in his new room the next morning. There was a pitcher and basin balanced on the windowsill, and a wooden chair wedged beneath the doorknob. No one else had tried to break in and kill him during the night.

He dressed and went to Bessie's to see if they were open for breakfast. They were, and apparently much of the town ate breakfast there. He had a short wait before he was shown to a table. The steak was so good the night before that he ordered steak and eggs.

He was working on his last cup of coffee when something occurred to him. His waitress was young and very pretty, and this was apparently one of the best places to eat in town.

This was Gerry Beck's kind of place.

"Excuse me," he said to the waitress as he paid her.

"Yes?"

"What's your name?"

"Lorna."

"Lorna, I'm looking for a friend of mine who was supposed to have passed through town in the last few weeks. Maybe you ran into him."

"Why do you think that?" she asked. "Wouldn't it be better if you checked with a bartender?"

"No," he said, "this is the kind of place he would have come. Good food, and a beautiful waitress."

She blushed. "You think I'm beautiful?"

Actually, she was young and pretty, but that was close enough for Beck.

"Of course I do," Lancaster said, "and my friend would, too. His name is Gerry . . . Gerry Beck."

Her eyes widened. "I know Gerry!"

"You do?"

"He was here for a few days, and he ate here every morning and every night."

"I thought so," Lancaster said.

She leaned in and said, in a low voice, "He even asked if he could take me to supper."

"And did he?"

"No," she said, as if the very idea was appalling. "He was . . . too old."

"He's my age."

148

"Really?" she said. "He looks older."

"Really?"

"Yes."

"But you did talk to him, right?" Lancaster asked.

"Well, of course," she said. "I had to be polite. My mother is Bessie."

"Bessie?"

"The owner? I have to be polite to the customers."

Like now, he thought.

"Well, I'm not gonna take up your time," he promised. "I just need to catch up to Gerry, and I was wondering if he told you where he was going after here."

"No."

"Can you give it some thought —"

"He didn't tell me exactly where he was going," she said. "But he did say he was going to Texas."

"Texas? Texas is a big place, Lorna. Did he tell you where in Texas?"

"He didn't say where," she said. "Or I don't remember. I'm sorry."

"Yeah, so am I," Lancaster said. He gave her the money for his breakfast and got up to leave. He was about to go out the door when she caught up to him and grabbed his arm.

"The panhandle."

"What?"

"He said he was heading for the Texas panhandle. Does that help?"

"Yes, Lorna," he said, "that helps a lot. Thank you."

The panhandle.

If Beck had said that to anyone but a young, pretty girl, Lancaster would have discounted it. Beck only lied to young women when he knew he was staying in town. So mentioning to Lorna that he was headed for the Texas panhandle was probably true.

Now all Lancaster had to do was get a lead on one of the other three — whichever of them came here to Henderson.

He had planned to check the whorehouse for Gerry Beck, but now that he'd found Lorna that wasn't necessary. On the other hand, Sweet or one of the others might have needed a whore, too. Lots of men did when they came in off the trail.

So he headed for the whorehouse.

THIRTY-FOUR

"Adderly."

"He was here?" Lancaster asked.

The girl looked at him and said, "That's what I just said. He was here."

There were two whorehouses in town, and this was the second. The girl was a pretty, slightly faded, and plump girl of about thirty. Her name was Angel. She was sitting on a bed with grimy sheets in a tiny room with one dirty window. Lancaster had seen cleaner campsites.

"His name is kinda weird," she said. "That's why I remember him."

"Adderly?"

"No, his first name," she said. "It's Chester."

"Chester."

"He said his friends called him Chet, but he wanted me to call him Chester while we did it."

"How many times was he here?"

"A few," she said. "He was in town for about a week, and then he left."

"Did he come by to say good-bye?"

"What the hell?" she said. "I'm a whore, I wasn't his girlfriend. Who says good-bye to a whore when they leave town?"

She was right, of course.

"Okay, thanks."

"Hey," she said as he turned to the door.

"What?"

"My money?"

"Oh, sorry." Lancaster gave her the money he'd promised her.

"Don't forget to tell that bitch downstairs what a good ride I gave you."

"I won't forget," he promised.

"Thanks."

He opened the door, but before leaving he asked, "Did Adderly go with any of the other girls?"

"One," she said. "He went with Lisa first, but after that he was with me, and he stayed with me. That Lisa, what a skinny bitch."

"Lisa," he said. "Thanks."

"Tell that bitch downstairs to send up the next one," she said.

"Right."

"Another one?" the bitch downstairs asked.

"Yeah, Lisa," Lancaster said.

152

"What, Angel wasn't enough for you?"

"Angel was great," he said. "Worth every penny. But then she told me about this skinny girl —"

"You like 'em skinny?"

Lancaster was getting impatient. He took out some money and shoved it into the woman's hand. "Look, I need to talk to Lisa. Five minutes. She knows something about a man I'm looking for."

She looked at the money in her hand. "For this you can talk for half an hour."

"Five minutes."

"Go ahead," she said. "Room three."

He started up the stairs, then turned and said, "Angel said to send up the next one."

"Already?"

"She's a helluva worker."

"I guess so," she said. "Okay."

He went up the stairs, walked to room three, knocked, and went in.

Lisa didn't know a thing about a man named Adderly.

"Oh, Chet!" she said, when he explained who he was looking for. "I didn't get his last name."

"You called him Chet? His name was Chester, right?" Lancaster asked.

"Yeah, but I called him Chet."

He could see her shoulder and hip bones

153

through the thin robe she was wearing. She was older than Angel, but either not as busy or cleaner, because the room — and the sheets — were not as grimy.

She screwed up her face.

"Maybe he didn't like that, because he never came back to me. Started using that bitch Angel."

"You don't like Angel?"

She wrinkled her nose and said, "She's dirty."

"Thanks for the warning."

"So you're lookin' for Chet?"

"Yeah."

"You gonna kill 'im?"

"Probably. What made you ask?"

"You look like a gunman," she said. "He looked like an outlaw." She shrugged. "I slept with so many men — cowboys, gunmen, gamblers, lawmen — that I can tell them apart."

"And can you tell me anything about him?" Lancaster asked.

"Like what?"

"Like where he was going when he left Henderson?"

"We didn't talk much," she said. "In fact, he was finished with me pretty quick."

"Sorry to hear it."

"No, no," she said, "those are the best

154

kind of customers, the ones who finish fast, roll over, break wind, and then leave. Well, except for customers like you."

"Like me?"

She nodded. "The kind who pay to talk."

"Oh." He took out the money he promised her and she shoved it into the pocket of her robe.

"Anything else I can do?" she asked.

"No," he said. "That's it. Thanks."

"Any time," she said. "Come back and talk some more."

"I don't think so," he said. "I'm leaving town."

"Too bad."

He started to leave but as he grabbed the doorknob she said, "Wait."

"What?"

"He asked me a question before he left."

"What question?"

She screwed her face up again. "He asked me if I knew a place called Peach . . . something."

THIRTY-FIVE

As promised Lancaster stopped in at the sheriff's office before leaving Henderson.

"Did you get what you wanted?" Carver asked.

"I've got a line on two of the men I'm tracking," Lancaster said.

"Well, congratulations, then," the lawman said. "I guess you're on your way, then."

"That's right."

"I'll walk out with you."

Out front the lawman saw Crow Bait tied off and was taken aback. "That's your horse?"

"That's right."

"Couldn't get somethin' better?"

"This horse carried me out of the desert, saved my life," Lancaster said. "I owe it to him to ride him for as long as I can."

"Don't seem it would be that long, from the look of 'im."

"He's better than he looks, believe me,"

156

Lancaster said, hoisting himself into the saddle. "Thanks for your help, Sheriff."

The sheriff knew he hadn't done anything, but he said, "Any time."

Lancaster knew he'd never be in Henderson again, so he just waved and turned Crow Bait east.

Next stop was Peach Springs, Arizona.

As Lancaster rode out of town, the sheriff went back into his office, took the cell key from the peg on the wall, and entered the cell block.

"He's gone," he said, while fitting the key into the lock.

In the cell Kent stood up impatiently.

"Come on out," Carver said.

Kent followed the lawman out of the cell block to his desk. There Carver returned Kent's hat and gun belt.

"You better warn Beck that Lancaster's comin'," Carver said.

Strapping the gun on, Kent said, "Don't worry, Gerry'll take care of 'im. I remember him now. Lancaster was a drunk for years. He's lost it."

"He took care of you and your partner," Carver said. "You're lucky you're not dead."

"Oh yeah? Well, next time's gonna be different," Kent said. "I'm gonna make him pay for killin' Tyler."

"Yeah, you do that," Carver said, sitting down.

"You don't think I can?"

"I'm just sorry I won't be there to see you try," Carver said.

"You got a big mouth, fat man."

"And you're about to talk yourself right back into a cell," Carver said. "Look, I'm done with Beck and I'm done with you and your kind. Now get out of my office and get out of my town."

Kent stood in front of the sheriff with his muscles bunched, his jaw twitching.

"Go ahead and try it," Carver said. "I didn't get to be this age by backin' down from the likes of you."

Kent stared at Carver with undisguised rage, but eventually his muscles relaxed and he backed down. "You're lucky I want Lancaster first."

Carver looked down at his desk and said, "I can't even hear you anymore, Kent. You're a memory to me. A bad memory."

THIRTY-SIX

Lancaster used the time it took to ride from Henderson to Peach Springs to bond further with Crow Bait. He spoke to him each night as he rubbed him down and fed him, and then made sure to give him some green apples for a treat. To his eye the horse did not seem to be putting on weight, but each day the animal seemed to be getting stronger. He still looked like a bag of bones, but he felt stronger.

And he swore the horse could understand him when he spoke to him. This was the most serene animal he'd ever ridden. Nothing seemed to faze him, whether they were on the trail or camped. They encountered a rattler at one point, and Crow Bait couldn't have cared less while Lancaster shot the reptile. And nothing in the darkness ever rattled the horse. Although Lancaster felt certain that, if there were any danger approaching, the animal would have sounded the alarm.

Lancaster swore that, for the rest of his life, he'd never judge anything by the way it looked — man or beast.

Peach Springs was a small town — what some people would call a "one horse" town. As he rode in he saw only three buildings — one was a hotel, one a saloon, and one a livery. He reined in Crow Bait in front of the hotel. As he walked in he smelled food cooking. He wondered if this was the one place in town to eat.

"Afternoon, friend," the clerk said. He was a man in his fifties with a smile that looked plastered on. Lancaster wondered if he smiled all night, while he was asleep.

"Good afternoon."

"Do you need a room?" the clerk asked. "We've got plenty. We don't get many visitors."

"Who's your kitchen cooking for, then?" Lancaster asked.

"Anyone who wants to eat," the man said. "Folks around here don't have any place else to go."

"I see. Well, I'll take a room, and then I'll come down to eat."

"Excellent," the man said. He turned, took

a key from the wall, and handed it to Lancaster.

"Do you want me to check in?" he asked.

"It's not necessary," the clerk said. "If you don't like the room, you can try another one. We have plenty."

"Thank you."

"The rooms are upstairs."

As Lancaster started for the stairs the clerk called, "What would you like to eat?"

"What are my choices?"

"Beef stew."

Lancaster waited, but when the clerk offered no alternative he said, "Beef stew will be great. I'll be down in a few minutes."

"Is your horse out front?" the man asked. "I can have it taken to the stable."

"That'd be helpful. Thanks."

"What does it look like?"

"You won't be able to miss it," Lancaster said, and went upstairs.

The man who brought him his bowl of beef stew looked just like the clerk, only a few years younger.

"My brother said you wanted stew."

"He didn't say I had another choice."

"He likes the stew," the waiter said. He put it down next to the basket of rolls he had brought earlier. It looked delicious and

161

smelled the same.

"This will do nicely," Lancaster said.

"Enjoy."

The man walked away and Lancaster broke a roll, dunked it in the stew, and tasted. It was just as good as it looked. For the next twenty minutes, all he concentrated on was eating that, and a second bowl.

"You were pretty hungry," the waiter said, collecting the second bowl.

"I didn't realize how hungry until I tasted your food," Lancaster said. "Tell me, does everyone in this area eat here?"

"Unless they eat at home," the waiter said.

"Who lives in the area?"

"There are quite a few ranches around us."

"Why isn't the town larger, then?" Lancaster asked. "Why don't you have a general store? Or a trading post?"

"The ranchers usually go to Audley or Seligman for their supplies," the waiter said.

"How far are they?"

"Thirty, and thirty-seven miles, thereabouts."

"But they come here to eat?"

"Unless they stay home."

"Yes, you said that."

"Would you like anything else?"

"Some more coffee."

"Comin' up."

A town this size didn't have much to offer. It didn't offer much cover, either. If he started asking questions about Chet Adderly, word would get around. He was going to have to figure out a way to get answers without asking too many questions.

Certain questions were harmless, though.

"What's your name?" he asked the waiter when he brought the coffee.

"George."

"And your brother?"

"Which one?"

"How many do you have?"

"Well," he said, "Harry is the cook, Fred is the desk clerk, and Sam runs the livery."

"Four brothers? And you pretty much run the town?"

George laughed and said, "We are the town."

"What about the saloon?"

"Our cousin Dan owns it, and he's the bartender."

"One big happy family, huh?"

"Except for our sister," George said. "She's not so happy."

"Why?"

"She hates it here. Wants to leave."

"Why doesn't she?"

"She doesn't have a man."

"She needs a man to leave here?"

George looked shocked. "A young lady can't travel alone."

"Oh, right," Lancaster said. "Uh, how old is your sister?"

"Hermione is forty."

"Hermione," Lancaster repeated. "Forty."

George nodded. "Is that all you want?"

"Yes," Lancaster said. "Everything was great. How much do I owe you?"

"Two bits."

Lancaster passed it over and said, "And worth every penny."

THIRTY-SEVEN

Lancaster found out the family last name of George, Harry, Fred, Sam, and Hermione was Dickson. Apparently, Hermione's age of forty made her the baby.

After the beef stew he walked over to the livery to check on Crow Bait.

"Not many men would give a horse like that a chance," the liveryman said as he entered.

"You're Sam, right?"

"That's right."

"I met your brothers George and Fred."

"You had the beef stew?"

"Yes, I did."

"It was good, huh?"

"It was better than good."

Sam wiped his hand on his trousers and stuck it out.

Lancaster shook it and said his name.

"Horse don't look like much, but he's strong," Sam said. "What's his name?"

165

"Crow Bait."

That made Sam laugh until he was bent over double, choking. "That's rich. You come to see if I'll take good care of him?"

"That's right."

"Well, don't you worry," Sam said. "He's in good hands. Why don't you go over to the saloon and have a drink?"

"And meet your cousin Dan, huh?"

"Dan," Sam said with a face that said he didn't like his cousin, "yeah."

"What's wrong with Dan?"

Sam shrugged. "He's a cousin, not a brother."

That seemed to be reason enough for the dislike.

"Well, I think I'll take your advice," Lancaster said. "I hope he's got cold beer."

"He's got it," Sam said. "We may be a small town, but we got everythin' you'll need." Sam raised his eyebrows, grinned, and added, "Everythin'."

Lancaster left the livery, wondering if "everything" meant sister Hermione?

Lancaster was unaware that he was being watched from a window on the second floor of the hotel as he crossed over to the saloon. The white lace curtain was pulled aside, remained that way until he entered the

166

saloon, then fell back across the window.

The saloon was empty, except for the bartender. If Lancaster hadn't been told that Dan was a cousin, he wouldn't have recognized him as family. He didn't look anything like the brothers. For one thing, they all had gray hair, while his was pitch-black.

"Welcome to the Peach Springs Saloon, friend," the bartender said.

"You're Dan, right?"

"Ah, I see you met my cousins already."

"I did."

"Well, belly up and tell me what your pleasure is."

"Beer," Lancaster said, "cold."

"Comin' up."

Lancaster took off his hat, set it on the bar, and ran his hands through his hair.

"Been ridin' long?" Dan asked, setting the beer down.

"Long enough." Lancaster took two swallows of the cold beer, closed his eyes as the cold ran through him. How easy it would be just to sit and drink, switch to whiskey, and just drift away . . .

"You must be passin' through," Dan said.

"Why do you say that?"

"That's all anybody ever does, pass through here. Nobody ever stops for more

167

than a day or two."

"And if they stop for a day or two, what is there to do?" Lancaster asked.

"Nothin'," Dan said, "nothin' at all."

"Your cousin Sam said I could get anything I want here," Lancaster said.

"Yeah, well," Dan said, "that depends on how bad you want it."

"Well, the food and the beer are good."

"If you like beef stew all the time," Dan said.

"Is that all your cousin Harry can make?"

"No," Dan said, "he can make bacon and eggs."

"Bacon and eggs and stew? That's it?"

"Rolls," Dan said. "He can bake rolls."

"Well, that's food and beer, anyway," Lancaster said. "What about . . . other things?"

"Can't get no supplies," Dan said. "I mean, we could probably sell you some cartridges, let you have some coffee and bacon for the trail."

"And that's it?"

"What else is there?"

"Women?"

Dan made a face.

"You can have a woman if you don't mind my cousin Hermione," Dan said.

"The boys pimp out their sister?"

"Don't let them fool you," Dan said. "Hermione is the one in charge."

"Really? I heard she was the baby of the litter."

"She's also the only one with any brains."

"What about you?" Lancaster asked. "You seem to have some brains."

"I'm only a cousin," Dan said. "Thank God."

"So Hermione whores herself out?"

"Don't let the smiles fool you," Dan said. "Any one of them will do anything to make a dollar."

Lancaster took another measured swallow.

"You want another?"

"No, this is good. So tell me, why would anyone actually come here? I mean, why would they purposely head here?"

"Here? To town?" Dan shrugged. "Beats me. Maybe they'd go to one of the ranches, but here?"

"Maybe," Lancaster said, "I should meet your cousin Hermione."

George turned to see who was coming down the stairs — not that it was any great mystery.

Hermione Dickson crossed to the desk and stared at her brother, whose smile seemed to freeze.

169

"Who's the man who just rode in?"

"Henry says his name is Lancaster."

"What did he want?"

"A room."

Hermione was not a large person. In fact, all of her brothers were physically larger than her, but they were cowed by her intelligence and the force of her personality.

"That's all?"

"That's all he asked for."

Hermione looked inward and said, "It don't make sense. He must be here for somethin'."

"Well," her brother said, "we got all night to find out what."

THIRTY-EIGHT

Lancaster nursed his beer.

Dan just stood behind the bar and watched.

"You ever get any other customers?"

"Sure," Dan said. "Some of the ranch hands come in once in a while, but there are a couple of saloons in Audley, more in Seligman."

"That's a long ride."

"Some of the ranches are halfway between here and Audley. Just as long a ride either way. More beer and women there."

That made coming to Peach Springs even more of a mystery. Maybe he was in the wrong place. Maybe there was another town with peach in the name. He posed the question to Dan.

"Not that I know of," the bartender said. "Not in Arizona, anyway."

"Why do you stay here?" Lancaster asked.

"Why?" Dan spread his arms. "I own all

this. If I go someplace else, I won't own nothin'."

"I guess you have a point there."

"Besides," Dan added, "Hermione won't let me go, and I'm as afraid of her as her brothers are. Maybe more, because I don't think she'd hesitate to kill me."

"I'm gettin' more and more curious to meet this woman."

"Oh, I'm sure you will," Dan said. "She's probably been watchin' you from on high."

"On high?"

"Second floor of the hotel, front," Dan said. "Hermione made sure she has the best room in the hotel."

"Down the hall from me?"

"Probably."

Lancaster pushed the beer mug away with a third of it still there.

"Somethin' wrong?" Dan asked.

"I've had enough," Lancaster said. "Since we're bein' so clear and honest with each other, Dan, let me ask you a question."

"Go ahead," Dan said, leaning his elbows on the bar. "Bartenders are good at answering questions."

"Well, maybe more than one," Lancaster said. "Have there been any other strangers in town in the past — oh, month or so?"

"Nope," Dan said. "None."

172

"You answered that one real quick."

"I think I'd notice if any strangers came to town."

"Yeah, I guess you would."

"Are you here lookin' for somebody?"

"I am looking for somebody," Lancaster said, "and I thought they might have passed through here."

"Why?" Dan asked. "Why would anybody come here?"

"For the beef stew?"

At that point the batwings opened and one of the brothers came in. At the moment, Lancaster didn't know which one it was.

"Hello, George."

"Dan."

"What are you doin' here?" Dan asked. "Why aren't you at the hotel?"

"No customers," George said. "So Hermione sent me over."

Dan gave Lancaster a "See, I told you so" look.

"Does she want me?" Dan asked. "Or our guest?"

George frowned at Dan and asked, "Why would she want to see you?"

THIRTY-NINE

Lancaster followed George back to the hotel and up to the second floor. Sam gave him a smile along the way. Going up the stairs, he remembered Dan telling him not to be fooled by their smiles.

He noticed that none of the brothers wore guns, so he didn't feel threatened. He didn't see any reason not to follow George up to Hermione's room. After all, she was in charge, and he probably should have been talking to her the whole time.

George led him down the hallway, past his room, to the door at the end of the hall. There they stopped, and George knocked.

"Come in," a woman's voice said.

George opened the door.

Lancaster was about to get his first look at Hermione Dickson, who seemed to be in charge of the entire town — all three buildings — of Peach Springs, Arizona.

"Hermione?" George said. His voice

quavered just a bit. "Mr. Lancaster is here."

"Get out, George," the woman said.

"Yes, Hermione." George gave Lancaster a look, then turned and went back up the hall.

"Come on in, Lancaster," Hermione said.

He walked in the door and saw her standing by the window. She was a tall, rawboned woman with short red hair, wearing a plain cotton dress that obviously had nothing underneath it. The kindest thing you could say about her was that she was a handsome woman. Not what you'd expect to find in a whorehouse or a saloon. He supposed if a man came to town looking for a woman, and Hermione was what he got, he could make it work.

"Close the door, please," she said.

He did.

"I been watchin' you since you came to town," she said.

"That a fact?"

"Oh yeah. You spent some time talkin' to my cousin Dan."

"He's a bartender," Lancaster said. "That's what you do with a bartender, you talk to him."

She stood framed in the window, the light coming in from behind her, making her dress almost transparent. She had to be aware of that, but she didn't have the body to give it the desired effect.

She folded her arms beneath her small breasts.

"Why did you come to Peach Springs, Lancaster?"

"I'm told men come here for the food, and the, uh, female companionship."

"You got a good look at me, right?" she asked, dropping her arms to her sides. "You think men come here for me? You didn't come here for me."

Lancaster gave it some quick thought. He had not seen a gun since he arrived, and certainly no one had made any kind of threatening move toward him. The entire town was made up of one woman, her four brothers, and their cousin — who seemed to be the smartest of the men. And he said he hadn't seen a stranger in town in over a month.

"Okay," Lancaster said, "okay, Hermione — uh, Miss Dickson."

"Hermione's good," she said. "Just Hermione."

He wondered why, with a name like that, she didn't have some sort of nickname.

"Hermione, I'm looking for a man named Adderly," he said. "I was told he was coming here to meet a man, named Cardiff."

176

"Cardiff?" she repeated. "You're lookin' for Cardiff?"

"Actually, I'm looking for three men," he said. "Adderly, Cardiff, and Sweet."

"I don't know anybody named Sweet," she said, "but I know Cardiff."

"Not Adderly? Chet Adderly?"

"No, not Adderly. Just Cardiff, Jim Cardiff."

"I don't know his first name," Lancaster said, "but Cardiff's not a common name, so it must be him. Where is he?"

"He's gone." She folded her arms again.

"Gone? Gone where?"

"Just gone. Let's talk about you. Did the boys tell you about the toll?"

"Toll? What toll? They didn't mention anything."

"Anybody who rides through Peach Springs has to pay a toll."

Lancaster wondered what the hell she was talking about.

"Hermione, we're getting off the point."

"No, we're not," she said. "The toll is the point. See, you can't leave town without payin' the toll."

"What toll?" Lancaster was getting frustrated. "Nobody said anything about a toll."

"George!" she suddenly yelled. The door opened and George appeared. "Nobody

177

told Lancaster about the toll?"

"Not yet, Hermione, dear."

"Why not?"

"We just didn't get to it yet."

"What if he don't have any money?"

"He's got money," George said. "I saw it when he paid for his beef stew. He'd got a lot of money."

Lancaster had kept his money on him, rather than leave it in his room. He still had most of the thousand dollars Andy Black had given him.

So that was it. They were after his money. But how did they expect to get it?

"Look," he said, "all I'm interested in is where Cardiff or Adderly went when they left here."

"When they left?" Hermione asked.

"That's right."

"You don't got to worry about that," she said. "Let's talk about the toll."

"Okay," he said, "let's get this out of the way. What about the toll? How much is it?"

"Half," she said.

"Half of what?"

"Half of whatever you have," she said.

"He's got a lot," George said again.

"George," she said, "go talk to your brothers."

"Talk to —"

178

"Go!"

"Oh," he said, as if he just got it. "Okay."

"Okay," she said, after George had gone, "how much have you got?"

"It doesn't matter how much I've got, Hermione," Lancaster said, "I'm not giving you any of it."

"In that case," she said, firming her jaw, "you've got a problem."

"What kind of problem?"

"If you don't pay our toll," she said, "you don't leave Peach Springs alive."

FORTY

Lancaster stared at her for a few moments, wondering if she was serious.

"Yes," she said.

"Yes, what?"

"You're wonderin' if I'm serious," she said. "The answer is yes."

"I'm also wonderin' how you're gonna enforce that threat," he said.

She smiled, and just for a moment she became pretty. He wished he could have seen her when she was in her twenties.

"I've got four brothers," she said.

"With no guns."

"They have guns," she said. "You just haven't seen them yet. And they know how to use them."

Lancaster studied her. She was dead serious. He'd been taken. Just because he hadn't seen any guns didn't mean there weren't any. Don't be fooled by the smiles.

"What about your cousin?"

180

"Dan? What about him? He's a cousin."

"He's a good bartender."

"That's about all he is," she said. "No, it's me and my brothers you have to worry about."

"Well," Lancaster said, "it's me you have to worry about. You're in this room with me, and I don't see a gun on you."

"You wouldn't shoot an unarmed woman."

"You don't know me."

"I've known a lot of men like you," she said. "They come here, they pay the toll, or they die."

"Not me," he said.

"What makes you so special?"

"I've got you," he said. "You're gonna get me out of here alive."

She smiled. "Look out the window."

She moved away from the window so he could walk to it. He kept one eye on her, just in case she had a gun hidden somewhere.

When he looked out the window, he saw the four brothers standing in the street in front of the hotel. They all wore guns on their hips.

"They know how to use them," she said.

"You said that already."

"No, I mean they really know how to use them."

"I guess we'll find out."

"So you're not gonna pay?"

"Not one penny."

"You're gonna walk out there?"

"With you," he said, "yes. You're gonna get me my horse and I'm gonna leave your little town. It's up to you and your brothers who's still alive when I do."

She stared at him. "Lancaster? That's your name?"

"Yes."

"Should I know that name?"

He could see it in her eyes. She was starting to think that maybe they had made a mistake this time.

"Probably not," he said. "Not if you've spent your whole life here, in this little town."

"I guess I should stick my head out once in a while," she admitted.

"Well," he said, "you're gonna stick your head out now. Come on, let's go."

FORTY-ONE

Lancaster walked Hermione down to the lobby at gunpoint. The desk was deserted, as all the brothers were in the street. He could sense that her mind was racing. She would come up with some kind of offer before they hit the street.

He was starting to think he might have been wrong when she stopped walking just before they got to the door.

"There's an easier way to do this," she said.

"How's that?"

"Pay the toll," she said. "I'll reduce it. As long as you pay something, the boys will let you leave."

"Out of the question," he said. "I won't pay anything."

"Why do you have to be so stubborn?"

"Let's just say it's my nature."

"What if I could give you what you came here for?" she asked.

"You said you couldn't."

"I lied."

"Why?"

"Let's just say it's my nature."

"Then why should I believe you now?"

"Because I'm tryin' to save us both a lot of trouble," she said.

"You should have thought of that before."

"Wait, wait," she said impatiently. She turned to face him. "Flagstaff."

"What about it?"

"You're lookin' for a man named Sweet," she said. "He's in Flagstaff. Or at least that's where Cardiff said he was goin'."

"And why would he tell you that?"

"Men talk in bed sometimes."

"You're telling me that Cardiff came here to have sex with you?"

"He liked it here," she said.

"And what about Adderly?"

"He didn't like it here."

"So they were both here?"

"Yes."

"But not now?"

"No."

Lancaster wasn't sure he could believe her, but there was someone else he could ask.

"Okay," he said, "let's go."

"Back upstairs?"

184

"No," he said, "outside."

"But . . . you have what you want."

"Sorry, Hermione, but I don't believe you," he said. "Come on. Out."

"B-but it's crazy."

"Are you trying to save yourself or your brothers?" he asked.

"I'm trying to save all of us!"

"I'm used to this kind of thing, Hermione," he said. "I made my living for years with my gun. This'll just be a stop for me on the way to the saloon."

"You're crazy," she said, shaking her head.

"I think it's pretty close which one of us is crazier."

Outside, the Dickson brothers waited confidently. They'd been through this many times before. Lancaster would step through the front door, and they'd gun him down easy. After that they'd empty his pockets of all that money George had seen.

But when Lancaster stepped out, he had Hermione in front of him, and none of the brothers was prepared for that.

From the saloon, Dan watched the proceedings from the batwing doors. When he saw Lancaster appear in the doorway with Hermione in front of him, he chuckled and shook his head.

"Lancaster . . ." he said.

FORTY-TWO

Lancaster stood back from Hermione, instead of standing right up on her. She might have been a woman, but he was willing to bet she had some tricks. He hadn't searched her, and it was possible she had a gun somewhere beneath her skirts. He would be ready for her if she did.

As they stepped out the door, he saw the four brothers standing shoulder-to-shoulder rather than fanned out, the way they should have been. They were probably used to facing men who wilted beneath their superior numbers, or had no experience in a gunfight. Neither was true of Lancaster.

"Hello, boys," he said.

"What're you doin'?" Sam asked. "Let Hermione go."

"I don't think so," Lancaster said. "Drop your guns on the ground."

The brothers exchanged glances with each other, but none looked capable of making a decision.

"What do we do, Hermione?" George asked.

Lancaster saw her shoulders rise and she took a breath, preparing to answer. But before she could, Dan came busting out of the saloon, shouting, "What do you think you should do, you idiots? Kill him!"

Galvanized into action by someone actually making a decision, the four men went for their guns.

"No!" Hermione shouted, much too late.

Lancaster's gun was already out, and he had a cool head. While the brothers were firing wildly, their bullets taking out windows to either side of Lancaster, he pushed Hermione down to the ground and fired off measured shots.

Sam was first. A bullet hit him in the chest, driving him back two steps before he toppled over backward.

Harry went next. A bullet in the belly folded him over, and he slumped to the ground.

A piece of hot lead struck George in the forehead and he was dead before he hit the ground.

Fred actually dropped to one knee, either from instinct or weakness in his legs. Whatever the reason, it didn't help him. Two slugs hit him in the chest and he keeled over dead as the sound of the shots echoed and died out.

Lancaster, with one shot left, turned his attention to Hermione, but if she had a gun beneath her skirts she had no chance to reach for it. Even pushed down to the ground as she was, one of her brothers' bullets had hit her in the face. She was on the ground, on her side, with the back of her head blown out.

Lancaster quickly ejected his spent shells and replaced them, because there was still one family member left.

He looked over at the saloon, but there was no one there. Dan had apparently gone back inside.

Lancaster stepped down into the street and crossed over to the saloon.

FORTY-THREE

As Lancaster entered the saloon, he had his gun in his hand. Dan was standing behind the bar with a rag over his shoulder.

"Beer?"

"Come out from behind the bar, Dan," Lancaster said.

"What for?" Dan asked. "They're all dead, right? It's over?"

"You got a gun back there?"

"Nope."

"I've gotta ask you to come out from behind there with your hands up."

"Okay, Lancaster, okay," Dan said. "Take it easy."

Dan raised his hands and walked out from behind the bar.

"What's goin' on?" Lancaster asked. "What was that about?"

"What? Oh, that? You mean outside?" Dan shrugged. "I just didn't want the boys to back down."

"You wanted me to kill them," Lancaster said.

"Well, yeah," Dan said. "It was my only way out."

"So now they're dead," Lancaster said, "and what have you got?"

"Me?" Dan said. "I've got everythin'." He spread his arms. "It's all mine."

"Yeah, all three buildings," Lancaster said. He decided Dan was no threat and holstered his gun.

"How about that beer? On the house," Dan said.

"Sure, why not?" Lancaster said. "And then I'll be on my way — unless you're gonna tell me you got some law here."

"Now that it's just me," Dan said, going around the bar, "I'm the law, so don't worry about a thing."

He drew a cold beer and slid it over to Lancaster.

"Hermione give you what you wanted?" the bartender asked.

Lancaster took a swallow and then said, "She claims I should go to Flagstaff, says Cardiff said he was going there to meet Sweet."

"Maybe she was tellin' the truth."

"How likely is that?"

"Not very," Dan admitted. "She was a liar,

191

but maybe you had her worried enough to tell the truth for a change."

"Wait a minute," Lancaster said. He put his beer down on the bar. "You told me you didn't see any strangers in town."

"I ain't."

"But Cardiff was here."

"Cardiff's been here before," Dan said. "He wasn't no stranger."

"What about Adderly?"

"Well, okay," Dan admitted, "but he was Cardiff's friend."

"He was still a stranger."

"Okay," Dan said, "so I lied about that, but I knew it would come down to you or them." The bartender leaned on the bar. "See, I recognized your name. I knew they picked on the wrong man to try that toll business with."

"Come on, Dan," Lancaster said, "you must know something that can help me."

"Well," Dan said, "I do know somethin'."

"What?"

"Finish your beer and then come out back with me and I'll show you," Dan said.

"What's out back?"

Dan smiled and said, "You'll see."

192

FORTY-FOUR

Lancaster finished his beer and followed Dan to the rear of the building. The bartender opened a back door and led the way out. When they got out there, Lancaster saw a bunch of crosses and wooden headstones.

"This is our Boot Hill," Dan said.

Lancaster looked out over the expanse of graves and said, "All these people used to live here?"

"At one time," Dan said, "we were a whole town. Then one day there was a fire. Most of the buildings burned down. A lot of the people were killed, and the rest left. Except for Hermione and the brothers."

"And you."

"I came later, but I been here for a while," he said. "But not all of these graves are people who used to live here."

"Who else is here?"

"People who wouldn't pay the toll," Dan

193

said. "Or people who just crossed Hermione."

"So the brothers put some people back here with their guns?"

"Take a walk with me."

They walked through the graveyard and when they got all the way to the back Dan stopped in front of two new-looking graves.

"There ya go," he said.

Lancaster looked and saw the names Cardiff and Adderly on the wooden crosses.

"She said they weren't here anymore," Lancaster said. "I guess this is what she meant."

"They killed Cardiff when Hermione was through with him," Dan said. "Then they killed Adderly when he came lookin' for Cardiff."

Lancaster remembered the beating they had administered to him along with Sweet.

"These were hard boys," he said. "I can't believe the brothers took them both."

"Separately," Dan reminded him, "and did you think they were dangerous when you got here?"

"No, I didn't."

"They act — acted — like four idiots who were run by their sister," Dan said. "Well, they were run by her and they were idiots, but they were dangerous when they worked

194

together. They were just no match for you. You presented them with a situation they had never seen before, and they panicked."

"So everybody's dead but me and you."

"And I'm okay with that," Dan said. "But I got somethin' else to tell you. Come back inside."

Once they were back at the bar, Dan offered Lancaster another beer, which he turned down.

"What's this other thing you've got to tell me?" he demanded.

"I heard Cardiff tell Hermione about Flagstaff."

"What?"

"I overheard them. She was playin' like she wanted him to stay, but he told her he had to meet somebody in Flagstaff."

"And he said the name?"

"He did," Dan said. "He said Sweet."

"And how about Adderly, when he got here? Any word about Sweet?"

"No," Dan said, "he didn't last very long."

Lancaster gave Dan a long look. "You wouldn't be as big a liar as your cousin Hermione, would you?"

"Nobody was as big a liar as her, but look. You just did me a huge favor. I got no reason to lie to you. Besides, I got one more favor to ask."

"What's that?"

"Would you help me bury my family before you leave?"

Lancaster found Dan's desire to bury his "family" odd. However, once they had dug all the graves, rolled the bodies in, and covered them up, Dan's final words over the graves sort of clarified things.

"Good riddance," he said.

Still not convinced that the last family member wasn't going to try to kill him, Lancaster was alert while he saddled Crow Bait to leave town. When he rode the animal out of the livery, he raked the rooftops and windows of the hotel and saloon with his eyes, looking for a rifle barrel. Satisfied that Dan was true to his word and wasn't going to try to kill him, Lancaster turned Crow Bait south and headed for Flagstaff, Arizona.

FORTY-FIVE

Flagstaff, Arizona
Lancaster rode into Flagstaff a week later, after a short stop in Seligman to outfit himself again.

That Flagstaff was a lively, busy town was obvious as he rode down the main street. He doubted that Sweet would still be there, but he hoped that he'd be able to get a lead on him. Also, he had to be very careful in his search, now that the other two men were dead. Sweet was his only connection to whoever had hired the three of them to strand him in the Mojave Desert.

The other good thing about Flagstaff was that it took him in the right direction, toward the Texas panhandle, where he hoped to get a line on Gerry Beck. After all, he had to earn the thousand dollars he'd already been paid, and the four thousand that had been promised to him.

There was no way he'd be able to go

through Flagstaff in one day, so he rode directly to the livery to get Crow Bait taken care of.

"Yeah, yeah," he said to the liveryman. "I've heard it all before. Just take good care of him."

"Yes, sir."

He left the livery and checked into the first hotel he came to, not paying any attention to its name. It didn't matter, and neither did the quality, he just needed a room. These days the only time he considered quality was when he was looking to eat.

Lancaster decided to play this straight. He left the hotel and went right to the sheriff's office. He decided that if Sweet heard he was looking for him he wouldn't run. No, he'd come after him. Judging from the beating in the desert, he'd bring help, but this time Lancaster would be ready.

He realized that much of his anger over what had happened in the Mojave Desert was directed at himself. He should have been more alert. It was how he had stayed alive all those years of living by the gun. Now that he was just drifting, taking it a day at a time and not hiring out, he'd lost his edge. Taking a beating from two men who'd managed to get themselves killed by a woman and her four idiot brothers was ample indication of that fact.

When he got to the sheriff's office, the door opened and a man rushed out, barreling into him.

"Oh, sorry," the man said. "Gotta watch where I'm walkin'. You lookin' fer me?"

"If you're the sheriff, I am," Lancaster said.

"That's me, Sheriff Manning. I'm on my way to City Hall for a meetin'. You wanna walk with me or wait to see me later?"

"I'll walk with you, if you don't mind," Lancaster said.

"Good. Let's go."

The sheriff was as tall as Lancaster, but took shorter strides when he walked. Might have had something to do with the fact that he carried about fifty pounds more, mostly around his middle and in his ass. Lancaster had no trouble keeping pace.

"What can I do for you?"

"I just got to town, and I'm lookin' for a man," Lancaster said.

"Bounty hunter?"

There was no indication in the lawman's voice how he would have felt if Lancaster had said yes. Lancaster had to decide if he wanted to make this a personal matter, or tell the man he was working for Wells Fargo.

"I'm working for Wells Fargo," he said.

"That a fact?"

"Yes."

"You got any paper that says that?"

"No, but —"

"So if we go over to the Wells Fargo office and I ask, they'll say yes?"

"Their man might have to send a telegram," Lancaster said, "but in the end, yeah, they'd confirm it."

They walked in silence for a few strides, and then the sheriff said, "I'm gonna believe you. What's your name?"

"Lancaster."

"Who you lookin' for, Lancaster?"

"Actually, two men," Lancaster said. "A man named Sweet, and another man named Beck, Gerry Beck."

"You got a first name on Sweet?"

"No," Lancaster said. "Apparently nobody knows."

"What about you?" the lawman asked. "You got a first name?"

"I don't use it."

"Fine," the man said with a shrug. "Man's got a right to call himself what he wants."

The sheriff turned to cross the street so abruptly that Lancaster had to stop to let a buckboard go by before he joined the man.

"So, Sweet and Beck?"

"That's right," Lancaster said.

"Can't say I know Beck, although I've heard of him," Manning said.

"What about Sweet?"

"That's not a common name," Manning said. "Yeah, we had a man named Sweet here a couple of weeks ago."

"When did he leave?"

"He was here about a week, so I'd say a week ago."

"Any idea where he went?"

"I don't, no," Manning said. "All I know is that I ran him out."

"Ran him out? Why?"

"Because he's a troublemaker, that's why." The lawman stopped walking. "This is City Hall."

"Well, okay, but can you tell me who Sweet might have spent time with?"

"Check the Broken Branch Saloon, and Maisie's whorehouse. I think he spent most of his time in those places."

"Thanks, Sheriff," Lancaster said. "I appreciate it."

"Watch yourself," Manning said. "He might have made some friends while he was here."

"Thanks for the warning, Sheriff."

Manning opened the door to go into the three-story brick City Hall building, but stopped short. "Let me know what happens, will ya? And when you leave town?"

"Sure," Lancaster said. "I'll check in with you."

"Obliged if you would," the lawman said, and went inside.

FORTY-SIX

Lancaster had some direction now, so he decided to take the time to have something to eat. He hadn't had a good meal since the beef stew in Peach Springs — the only memorable thing about that visit, unless you call killing four men memorable. The meal he'd had during the few hours he was in Seligman left much to be desired.

He stopped into a saloon for a beer and some advice from the bartender on where to eat.

"Got a few good places in town," the young man said, "but my pick is Jilly's. Go out the door, turn left, and walk two blocks. It's small, but really good."

"Thanks."

"Ain't you gonna finish the other half of your beer?" the bartender asked.

"Half is good for me," Lancaster said. "Thanks."

■ ■ ■ ■

After a good steak at Jilly's, he went to the Broken Branch, the saloon the sheriff had said Sweet frequented while he was in town. If it wasn't the largest, busiest saloon in town, it had to be close. Somebody was pounding on a piano in the corner — badly — while girls worked the floor, bringing drinks to men who were either gambling or just sitting at tables, laughing and drinking.

The bar was crowded, but as usual Lancaster was able to find a space big enough for him. He got the bartender's attention, ordered a beer, then proceeded to nurse it while listening to the conversations going on around him. In a bar this crowded, there was no point in starting to ask questions about a man named Sweet. It made more sense to wait for the place to empty out some. The only thing was, he didn't think he could nurse one beer that long.

Of course, it would take a lot less time to question women than men, since there seemed to be about five girls working the floor. Maybe one of them would remember.

He still decided to wait a while, though. He'd attracted a little attention entering as a stranger. Better to give the novelty some time to wear off, give people a chance to forget that he was there.

There were two bartenders working the long bar, and he noticed one of them watching him. The man was experienced, in his forties, with eyes that saw everything. He noticed Lancaster was taking a long time to finish one beer, so Lancaster called him over.

"Can I get a fresh one?" he asked. "This has gone kind of warm."

"Sure thing."

The man drew him a fresh beer and brought it over.

"Don't let that one go warm," he advised.

"I'll try not to," Lancaster said, "but two is usually my limit. I'm afraid I'll have to make this one last."

"Well," the bartender said, "you only drank half of the first one, so you got another half to go."

There were too many customers for the bartender to spend too much time with one, but Lancaster noticed the man kept an eye on him even while serving others. A man like that would notice everything that happened around him. Lancaster might not have to ask anyone questions if he started with the bartender.

But the barman would be busy most of

the night. Lancaster decided to finish the beer and head over to the whorehouse. Maybe somebody there would be able to give him something.

"Leavin'?" the bartender asked. "How about that other half a beer?"

"I'll be back for it," Lancaster said.

The bartender nodded, and Lancaster left.

FORTY-SEVEN

Maisie's was a two-story building that had seen better days. Shutters were either hanging or missing, but all the windows were intact, and they were clean. There were other buildings in the area the same age, but in a more advanced state of disrepair. Lancaster had a feeling the rent was cheaper than somewhere else in town.

Lancaster entered and was immediately approached by the madam.

"Are you Maisie?"

"That's me, honey," she said. She had heavy makeup on her face to try to hide her wrinkles, but unsuccessfully. The fact that she was closing in on sixty was obvious. "What kind of girl do you like?"

He decided to play this differently than he had done in Henderson.

"I'm tracking a man. I understand he was in town a couple of weeks ago, and I know he likes prostitutes. Somebody told me you have the best girls in town."

"Well, that's true," she said. "What's your man look like?"

"Average-lookin', but his name is Sweet. I'm hoping one of your girls will remember him."

"Don't bother," she said. "He was here — twice. After that I banned him."

"Why?"

"He hurt one of my girls."

"Which one?"

"Her name was Carla."

"Was?"

"She's gone," Maisie said. "Left town right after that. Might have left the business, too."

"When did she leave?" Lancaster asked.

"A few days after the sheriff ran Sweet out of town," she said.

"Where'd she go?" he asked. "Do you know?"

"Why?"

Lancaster shrugged. "I'm just curious."

Maisie gave him a long look.

"You're good at this," she said. "You think maybe she liked bein' hurt and followed him?"

"It's possible."

She frowned at him.

"Haven't you ever known women who

208

liked being hit?" he asked.

"Unfortunately," she said, "yes."

"What about this one?"

"She wasn't here long enough for me to get to know her that well," Maisie said, "so I can't say."

"Was Carla her real name?"

"Yeah. She was new to the business, so she used her real name."

"Did she make any friends?"

"Not one," Maisie said. "Nobody liked her."

"All the more reason she might have followed him," Lancaster said.

"You married?" she asked.

"No."

"I'm not surprised."

"Why not?"

"You seem to know women too well for one to want to live with you."

"Well," he said, "I've never been accused of that before. And I don't really lead the kind of life a woman would want to share."

"You like the hunt too much, huh?"

"No," he said. "This is personal."

"Got anything to do with the cut over your eye?"

"Definitely. I don't suppose Sweet said anything while he was here that you might've heard, that would tell me where he went?"

"No," she said, "but Carla did say somethin'."

"What?"

"She said she thought she might do better for herself someplace like Amarillo."

Amarillo, he thought.

The Texas panhandle.

He left the whorehouse with a good feeling. All he needed was something from the bartender to confirm that Sweet headed for Texas. The man watched and he listened. If Sweet said anything useful, the bartender would have heard it.

As he was approaching the saloon again, he noticed the sheriff coming from the other direction.

"Lancaster," he said.

"Sheriff."

"A minute of your time?"

"Why don't we go inside —"

"Too noisy," Sheriff Manning said. "Let's talk out here."

"Okay," Lancaster said. "Okay."

FORTY-EIGHT

"What's on your mind?" Lancaster asked.

"I talked to Abe Walker," Manning said. "He's the Wells Fargo man here."

"And?"

"He confirmed what you told me," Manning said.

"Okay."

"But you told me you're trackin' a man named Sweet?" Manning said. "He only knows that you were hired to find a man named Beck."

"I told you that," Lancaster said. "I gave you both names."

"Yeah, but you told me you were tracking both of them for Wells Fargo."

"I don't think I really said that, Sheriff."

"Well, you led me to believe it."

"If I did, sorry," Lancaster said.

"What's this about Sweet?"

"He and a couple of partners were hired to kill me," Lancaster said. "They almost succeeded."

"So you're hunting them."

"Him," Lancaster said. "Sweet."

"What about the others?"

"They're dead."

"Killed by you?"

"No," Lancaster said. "They got killed before I could find them."

"So you need Sweet to find the man who hired him."

"Right."

"Any leads yet?"

"There's a bartender in here who's real observant," Lancaster said. "I'm gonna ask him what he knows."

"What about Maisie's?"

"I went there. Sweet was only with one girl, and she left town."

"Oh yeah," Manning said. "Hurtin' that girl was the last straw. That's when I ran him out."

"What was the first straw?"

"He started some trouble here," Manning said. "Got into a fight."

"With who?"

"Another stranger," Manning said. "He left town the next day."

"Damn."

"But your bartender might be able to tell you more," the lawman said. "Which one are you talkin' about?"

"I don't know his name, but he looks real experienced."

"Probably Ray," Manning said. "Tell him I said he should help you any way he can."

"Thanks, I will."

"I've got to finish my rounds," Manning said. "Maybe I'll see you later."

"Right."

Lancaster watched the sheriff walk off, then went through the batwings into the Broken Branch Saloon.

Lancaster got himself a spot at the end of the bar this time. It was away from a lot of the action, probably the quietest place in the saloon. The bartender brought him his beer and said, "On the house."

"I only had half comin'," he reminded the man.

"That's okay," the bartender said. "Drink however much of it you want."

"Are you Ray?" Lancaster asked.

The bartender had been in the act of turning away. He stopped short and looked at Lancaster.

"That's right," he said. "How'd you know?"

"The sheriff told me," Lancaster said.

"Why would he do that?"

"He said you could help me."

"With what?"

"I'm looking for somebody."

"Bounty hunter?"

"No," Lancaster said, "this is personal."

"Anythin' to do with that scar over your eye?"

"Yes."

"So, who you lookin' for?"

"A man named Sweet," Lancaster said. "The sheriff told me he caused some trouble in here a couple of weeks ago."

"Well," Ray said, "we did have some trouble, but we always have some trouble. What makes you think I can tell one trouble-maker from another?"

"Because you've been at this job a long time," Lancaster said. "You notice things — like me only drinking half a beer."

"Well," Ray said with a grin, "when a fella orders a beer and doesn't drink it all, that's kinda obvious."

"Still," Lancaster said, "I think you notice things that aren't so obvious."

"Like what?"

"Like a man like Sweet looking for trouble," Lancaster said. "Talkin' too loud at the bar? Maybe sayin' somethin' about where he's headed."

Ray leaned on the bar and pulled on his

lower lip. "Sweet, Sweet . . . Sheriff ran him out of town, right? Damaged one of Maisie's girls?"

"That was the story," Lancaster said.

"Whataya mean?"

"The girl may not have been so damaged," he said. "Looks like she might have followed him."

"To where?"

"That's the question," Lancaster said. He didn't want to put any ideas into the bartender's head by mentioning Texas.

"Well, gimme some time to think about it and maybe somethin' will come to me."

"I can give you some incentive —" Lancaster said, reaching into his pocket.

"No, no," Ray said, "I ain't tryin' to squeeze ya. If the sheriff said I can help ya, then I will — if I can."

"Okay," Lancaster said. "Then I'll check back in with you tomorrow."

"When do you wanna leave town?" Ray asked.

"Tomorrow."

"So no pressure, huh?"

"Just whatever you can do for me, Ray."

Ray gave Lancaster a salute and went back to work. Lancaster finished off his beer and turned in.

FORTY-NINE

In the morning Lancaster went to the livery to make sure Crow Bait would be ready to travel.

"Hey, mister," the liveryman said, "your horse just about ate me outta oats."

"He's got a good appetite."

"I know! And it don't show on 'im. But don't you worry, I'll have him ready to travel."

"Much obliged. Maybe about midday."

He left the livery and went back to Bessie's for breakfast. The young waitress served him but didn't make any conversation.

After breakfast he figured he had two stops to make. He had to talk to Ray and to Sheriff Manning. He had to talk to Manning first, because the Broken Branch wasn't open yet.

As he entered the sheriff's office, he was struck by how cramped it was.

"I know," Manning said, when he saw the

look on Lancaster's face. "They're supposed to be building a new jail. That's why I was goin' to a meeting yesterday."

"How'd it come out?"

"Not good," the lawman said. "Half the town council thinks they need a church. Another church."

"Too bad. What's the other half say?"

"That's what the mayor is workin' on. You come to say good-bye?"

"Almost," Lancaster said. "I still have to talk to Ray this morning. What time's the Broken Branch open?"

"Ten, but hell, go over and bang on the door. He's usually in earlier to clean the place up and get it set up for the day."

"Thanks," Lancaster said. "The quicker I talk to him, the sooner I can be on my way."

"I hope you find what you're lookin' for," the lawman said.

"I will," Lancaster said.

"You sound sure."

"I am," Lancaster said, "because I won't stop until I do find them."

He left the sheriff's office, crossed over to the Broken Branch, and banged on the locked door.

Ray opened the door and peered out at Lancaster through one good eye. The other one was swollen shut.

217

"Hey, come in," he said, backing away. "You want some breakfast?"

"I ate," Lancaster said. "What happened to your eye?"

"I ran into two friends of Sweet's last night," he said.

Lancaster followed him to a table in the back, where he was eating ham and eggs.

"Coffee?" Ray offered.

"Yeah, I'll take a cup."

Ray got up, went behind the bar, and came back with another cup, which he filled from the pot already on the table.

"Anyway, I was askin' some questions about your man Sweet —"

"I didn't want you to get in trouble, Ray," Lancaster said. "I just wanted you to see what you could remember."

"Well, I was askin' anyway, and apparently your boy Sweet's got friends all over the place. These boys heard I was askin' and they paid me a visit. Jumped me outside when I left for home. Said I better stop askin' questions if I knew what was good for me."

"Then what happened?"

"Well, I gave as good as I got, and they ran off. Guess they figured me for an easier mark."

"Know who they were?"

"Strangers passin' through," Ray said. "Not even here for a day. You know what I think?"

"What?"

"I think they're on their way to meet Sweet," Ray said.

"And you don't know their names?"

"Sorry."

"What'd they look like?"

Ray described two men who could have been outlaws or cowpokes. There was nothing unusual about them except for one thing.

"One of them was wearing a big silver ring on his right hand," Ray said, pointing to his eye. "That's how I got this."

"Silver ring," Lancaster said. "That's better than nothing. Thanks, Ray."

"I figure they stayed the night and left this mornin'," Ray said. "You can check at the livery when you pick up your horse."

"I'll do that. Hey, let me give you something for that eye."

"Give me enough to buy a steak."

"To put on your eye?"

"No, for supper tonight," Ray said. "I love a good steak smothered in onions."

Lancaster passed over some money and said, "Here, have two."

■ ■ ■ ■

Lancaster picked up Crow Bait and asked the liveryman about two men leaving earlier that morning.

"Sure thing," he said. "Looked like they been in a dustup, too. All bruised and such."

"Did they say anything about where they were going?" Lancaster said. "Maybe something they didn't know you could hear?"

"All I heard them say was that they better get their asses goin'," the liveryman said. "They had to meet some other fella."

"Did they say where?"

"No," he said, "but they rode west."

"West? You sure?"

"I know which way is west, young feller."

"I'm sure you do," Lancaster said. "Can you tell me anything about their horses?"

"Like what?"

Lancaster took a few dollars from his pocket and handed them over to the startled man. "Like anything that might help me track them?"

"Well, now that you mention it," the liveryman said, "their horses coulda used some new shoes. . . ."

FIFTY

Lancaster rode out of Flagstaff, heading west. There was no guarantee that these two men were on their way to meet with Sweet, but he wasn't losing anything by riding after them.

There were any number of towns in the Texas panhandle, but heading there usually meant Amarillo. Lancaster had been through Amarillo before, but he hadn't been there long enough to make any lasting friendships. Actually, he didn't make lasting friendships most places he went, but neither had he left behind any lasting acquaintances. He was going to be on his own when he got there, unless he once again tried to bring in the local law. So far, though, the local lawmen he'd encountered had not filled him with any sort of confidence.

It was also too much of a coincidence to think he'd find both Sweet and Gerry Beck in Amarillo at the same time.

So he figured to follow the tracks described to him by the liveryman as long as they kept heading west. In the event they veered off, he'd have to make a decision.

He found their sign not far out of Flagstaff. He could see what the liveryman meant about their horses needing new shoes. It made them easy to track. He took up a leisurely pace with Crow Bait, not wanting to catch up to the two men.

He camped each night, not bothering with a cold camp. He made sure he wasn't close enough for the two men to smell his coffee. And even if they did, what would they care? As far as he knew, they weren't running from anyone; they were simply riding, possibly to join up with Sweet. Besides, they'd be making their own coffee, so they probably wouldn't smell his. He had some dried meat with him, and some canned goods, all in his saddlebags. In the old days he had traveled light, and old habits die hard. He usually restocked whenever he came to a large town, bypassed the smaller towns. By their tracks, the two men were doing the same.

He restocked after three days, and then four. Each time he discovered that the two men had come before him, purchased supplies, and caused no trouble. After the dustup in Flagstaff, maybe they were keeping their noses clean.

Amarillo was about six hundred miles from Flagstaff. He and the three men were keeping a sensible pace. They'd probably get there three full days ahead of him, according to the temperature of their camps when he reached them. But the entire trip would take a few weeks — perhaps a little less — unless they increased their pace toward the end.

Lancaster and Crow Bait were becoming fully bonded as horse and rider. He talked to the animal while they rode, and again at night when they camped. Crow Bait was responding to the sound and tone of his voice. The animal could sense when Lancaster was relaxed, or when he was agitated. The horse took on a similar mood.

In each town they stopped in, Lancaster had to listen to disparaging words about his horse. It was starting to grate on him. At some point some big mouth was going to have to pay for the insults of others.

So far he'd been able to hold his temper. But who knew for how much longer?

FIFTY-ONE

Amarillo, Texas

Amarillo was young, but already booming as the old West headed for the twentieth century. The site had been chosen by J. T. Berry along the tracks of the Forth Worth and Denver City Railroad, which extended through the panhandle. The town was already the county seat, and had become a fast-growing cattle market because of its railroad and freight service.

As Lancaster rode down the town's main street, he saw that they had a Wells Fargo office. He bypassed it, but would stop in later to talk to the agent in charge.

The town had more than one livery stable. He picked one for no particular reason, withstood the eye-rolling of the liveryman when he saw Crow Bait.

"Got some nice horses you could look at before ya leave town," the man said to him.

"No, thanks, I'm satisfied with my horse."

"Really?"

"Just keep him well fed and cared for," Lancaster said.

"Yes, sir."

"Any other strangers in town in the past few days?" he asked.

"Lots."

Lancaster gave what little description he had of Sweet.

"That could be a lot of men, mister," the liveryman said. "Why you lookin' for this jasper?"

"Friend of mine," Lancaster said. "Supposed to meet up with him and a couple of other friends." He described the two men who had fought with Ray, the bartender.

"Again, could be anybody, and they might not have left their horses here."

"Yeah," Lancaster said, "thanks."

"Want I should recommend a hotel?"

"No, thanks," Lancaster said. "I'll pick that out myself."

"Suit yerself."

"I always do," Lancaster said. "Take care of that horse."

"That's my business, mister," the man answered. "I'll take care of 'im like he's my own."

"See that you do."

■ ■ ■ ■

Lancaster came out of his hotel into the chaos that was Main Street's traffic. Buckboards, freight wagons, riders and their horses pretty much choked the street. The foot traffic on the boardwalks was also heavy, and several times he had to step aside for ladies who were rushing somewhere. Men probably smelled that he was on the hunt, for they stepped aside for him.

Walking the streets, checking hotels, boardinghouses, and saloons would take forever. He wasn't sure that talking to the local Wells Fargo agent, or the local law, would be any kind of shortcut, but he had to try something. So far, in his search, he had not run across a lawman who impressed him. A good sheriff or marshal knew when strangers came to his town, and he checked them out. If that was the case in Amarillo, it would solve his problems, but he finally decided to go to the Wells Fargo office first. Maybe the agent there would be able to fill him in on what kind of law the town had.

He had passed the office on the way into town, so he knew where it was and headed over there.

FIFTY-TWO

At the Wells Fargo office he was surprised to find five men there. They were in a heated discussion with the agent, who Lancaster assumed was the man behind the desk. When he entered, all the men paused to look at him. Several of them continued to study him while one of them turned back to the agent and continued to berate him.

"If you think this is acceptable, then you're sadly mistaken, Turner," the man said. He was older than the others, about fifty, with steel gray hair and a tree trunk body. "My boys here are ready to take you apart if I give the word."

"Now, look, Mr. Atkins," the agent said, "there's no need for that. You set these boys of yours on me and somebody's bound to get hurt. That doesn't get you what you want, does it?"

"If what I want is to see you get hurt, it does," the man said.

"Don't do it, Atkins," the agent, Turner, said.

To Lancaster the man looked like he could handle himself in a fight, but the odds were four-to-one. Since Lancaster was technically working for Wells Fargo, he felt more than entitled to take a hand.

"Excuse me," he said.

All faces turned to him. The spokesman, Atkins, was scowling.

"Just a second, fella," he said. "I got business here."

"Sounds to me like you're just making threats, mister," Lancaster said. "Doesn't sound like business to me."

"Mister, you oughtta mind your own business," Atkins said.

"I am minding my business," Lancaster said. "I work for Wells Fargo. You got a beef with Mr. Turner here, you got a beef with me."

"Turner?" Atkins asked. "You know this fella?"

"Not by sight," Turner said, "but I got a feeling his name is Lancaster. That right, friend?"

"That's right, Mr. Turner. I assume you got a telegram about me?"

"Yes, sir," Turner said. "Nice to see you — especially right about now."

"Wells Fargo hirin' gunmen now?" one of the other men asked.

"Shut up, Wiley."

"Lemme take 'im, Mr. Atkins," Wiley said. He was about thirty and anxious to die, apparently.

Atkins studied Lancaster, as if he was considering letting his boy go, but in the end he just shook his head.

"Son," he said to Wiley, "this man would chew you up. You and the boys wait outside."

"But, boss —"

"Just do like I say, boy!"

Wiley gave Lancaster a hard look, which Lancaster returned with a languid look of his own. The other two men actually pushed Wiley out the door.

"This ain't over, Turner," Atkins said.

"I didn't think it was, Mr. Atkins."

Atkins walked up to Lancaster and fronted him. They were eye-to-eye. As thick as the man was, he was taller than he had first looked.

"You just get to town?" he asked.

"That's right."

"Tryin' to earn your money already?"

"I just came in to report to Mr. Turner," Lancaster said. "You seemed to be makin' an ass out of yourself, so I thought I'd save

229

you from yourself."

"You got a mouth on you."

"My mother used to tell me that."

"Your mother should've warned you to stay out of other people's business," Atkins said. "Next time I see you, maybe I'll let Wiley have a go at you."

"You were right," Lancaster said. "I would chew him up, and you'd be minus a man."

"Oh, he won't be alone."

"He wasn't alone today, either," Lancaster said.

"Two cowpokes weren't gonna back his play," Atkins said. "Next time will be different."

"Time for you to leave, Mr. Atkins," Lancaster said. "Me and Mr. Turner have official business."

Atkins glared at Lancaster for a few moments, then walked past him and out of the office, slamming the door behind him.

FIFTY-THREE

Turner let out a breath as Lancaster approached his desk.

"Most days like that?" Lancaster asked.

"Pretty much," Turner said, "but Atkins is one of the bigger mouths around here. Unfortunately, he's also one of the richest men."

"Yeah, well, in my experience those two pretty much go hand in hand." He stuck out his hand. "Lancaster."

"Bud Turner," the man said, shaking his hand. "Thanks for the help."

"I thought you could've handled that character Wiley, but four-to-one odds is too much for any man to have to handle."

"He would've set them on me, too," Turner said. "They wouldn't have killed me, but I would have taken a beatin'. Thanks again."

"Sure thing."

"Any word on Gerry Beck?" Turner asked,

sitting down.

"Well, I did hear that he was headed this way, but he could've been here and gone by now. I'm also tracking a man named Sweet."

"I heard. Somethin' personal, right?"

Lancaster touched the scar over his eye and said, "That's right."

"Won't let that get in the way of your Wells Fargo business, will you?"

"I'll do what I'm being paid to do."

"Speakin' of which, you think Beck is around here? Or was?"

"Possibly," Lancaster said. "But I just trailed two men here who may be meeting with Sweet."

"Any chance Sweet is meetin' up with Beck — or is that too much of a coincidence?"

"That's way too big a coincidence for me to even consider," Lancaster said. "Bad enough I have to deal with the coincidence of both of them even coming here."

"So what's your plan?"

"Well, I was going to talk to the local sheriff, but I wanted you to fill me in on him."

"His name's Jimmy Jacobs," Turner said. "Career lawman on the way out. Be sixty next year. I think he's gonna retire then."

"Honest?"

"As the day is long."

"So I can trust what he says?"

"Pretty much, although he may remember you from the old days, given his age."

"I'll chance it," Lancaster said. "If I need it will you vouch for me?"

"Wells Fargo will."

"Good enough."

Lancaster stood up.

"Hey."

"Yeah?"

"When you walked in," Turner said, "you sized up the situation pretty good."

"Well," Lancaster said, "I saw you facing four men, and didn't think you were threatening them. It wasn't that hard to pick a side."

"Well, thanks for pickin' mine."

"No problem," Lancaster said. "If you run into any more trouble while I'm in town, give me a holler and I'll help if I can."

"Much obliged," Turner said.

As Lancaster reached the door, Turner called, "Come by the Red Ribbon Saloon later and I'll buy you a drink."

"Red Ribbon?"

"It's owned by a woman."

Lancaster nodded and went out.

FIFTY-FOUR

Lancaster made his way across the crowded street and found the sheriff's office. Seemed like all he was doing of late was going from the Wells Fargo offices to the sheriff's office every time he hit a new town. He wanted to have this job over with.

"Sheriff Jacobs?"

The man behind the desk was tall and lean, gray haired with eyes to match, and a heavily lined face. He seemed to wear his career as a lawman on that face.

"Help ya?"

"I just came from the Wells Fargo office," he said. "My name's Lancaster."

"Lancaster." It was as if he were tasting the name. "Seems familiar."

"Maybe I can save you some trouble," Lancaster said. "The Chancellorville Revolt? That was me. The Fort Vincent War? Me."

"That Lancaster!" the man said.

"Yes."

234

"Well," the lawman said, "what war are you fighting around here?"

"I didn't know there were any wars around here."

"Oh, several. Unfortunately for you, wars these days are fought less with guns and more with words. Actually, that's unfortunate for you and me. See, we're dinosaurs, Mr. Lancaster, as we head for a new century."

"Well, Sheriff, I can tell you I ain't looking forward to a new century."

"You're younger than me," Jacobs said. "You'll still be young enough to enjoy it. Me? I'm not even sure I'll be around."

The two men stood there, several feet apart, alone with their own thoughts for a few seconds.

"Well," Jacobs said, breaking the silence, "what can I do for you, sir?"

"I'm doin' some work for Wells Fargo," Lancaster said. "Tracking Gerry Beck."

"Have a seat," Jacobs invited. "Beck's been hittin' them hard, I hear."

"Hard enough to pay me to track him."

"And you've tracked him here?"

"This direction, yeah," Lancaster said. "And he might be meeting up with a few other men."

"Like who?"

"Well, I've only got one name. A man called Sweet. Ring a bell?"

"Sweet." Jacobs thought a moment. "Can't say I recognize it."

"There's two more. But I don't know their names."

"And all trails have led you here?"

"That's right."

"Well, feel free to look around," Jacobs said. "I'll keep my eyes and ears open. We have had some strangers in town lately, but then we always have strangers in town. It's that kind of place."

"You have some deputies?"

"Two," he said. "Young, both of them, but I think one of them is gettin' ready to run against me next election. Probably beat me, too."

"You don't sound very confident."

"I've had my time," Jacobs said. "Might be time for some new blood."

"How old are you?"

"Be sixty soon."

"That ain't old, Sheriff."

"Yes, Mr. Lancaster," Jacobs said. "It is."

Lancaster stood up.

"If I find my man — or men — can I count on you for support?" he asked.

"If they've broken the law, it would be my job to aid you. So yes, you can."

236

"I appreciate it."

Before he could say any more, the door opened and two men walked in. Both were young — one in his late twenties, the other early thirties. Both were wearing deputy's badges.

"Sheriff," one of them said.

"Ah, boys," Jacobs said. "This is Mr. Lancaster. He's here tracking Gerry Beck for Wells Fargo. These are my deputies, Lyle and Bodeen."

Both men nodded at him, and Bodeen said, "The Chancellorville Revolt? That Lancaster?"

"That was me," Lancaster said.

"Damn," Lyle said.

"I've promised Lancaster our support if he runs into his men here."

"Men?" Bodeen asked.

"I'll explain it to you both," Jacobs said. "Lancaster was just leaving."

"Thanks for your help, Sheriff," Lancaster said on his way out.

"He's trouble," Bodeen said, when Lancaster left.

"Whataya mean?" Lyle asked.

"Wherever he goes there's a war," Bodeen said, "and if there ain't, he finds one."

"You're talkin' about the old days,

Bodeen," Jacobs said.

Bodeen was the deputy Jacobs thought wanted to be sheriff.

"I hope you're right, Sheriff," Bodeen said, "but if you don't mind, I'm gonna keep an eye on him."

"That's your job, Bodeen," the sheriff said.

"Right."

Bodeen left and Lyle looked at Jacobs.

"He wants your job, you know," Lyle said.

"I'll tell you a secret, Lyle." Jacobs held his thumb and forefinger about an inch apart. "I'm this close to tellin' him he can have it."

FIFTY-FIVE

Lancaster could feel the deputy behind him. It was the older one, Bodeen.

He knew the young man was watching him to see what kind of trouble he might get into, but that suited him. If he ran into Sweet or the other two or — even better — Gerry Beck, he knew this deputy would take a hand. He was the ambitious one.

Lancaster needed to find somebody in Amarillo who knew Beck or Sweet. Or he needed to find those two strangers.

And then it hit him. Probably the one man who could tell him where to find those two.

He turned a corner, then stepped into a doorway and waited. Moments later Deputy Bodeen came walking around the corner, and he stepped out. Bodeen stopped short, eyes wide.

"Hey!" Bodeen said.

"Buy you a drink, Deputy?" Lancaster asked.

Bodeen agreed to the drink out of curiosity and took Lancaster to the Red Ribbon Saloon.

They stopped in front and Lancaster looked up at the sign over the door, which had a red ribbon painted on it.

They went inside. It was the middle of the afternoon and the place was full.

"I'll get a table," Bodeen said, "unless you wanna talk someplace quieter?"

"No, this'll do," Lancaster said. In a place this noisy, there was probably less chance of them being overheard.

Lancaster waited by the door until Bodeen returned with two beers and said, "Come on."

He had actually gotten them a table in a small back room that was used for poker. He pulled the curtained doorway closed behind them.

"What's on your mind, Mr. Lancaster?" he asked as they sat.

"The sheriff told me one of his deputies was getting ready to run against him for his office in the next election," Lancaster said. "I figure that's you."

"What makes you think that?"

"You seem the ambitious type to me."

"Why not Lyle?"

"He didn't know who I am," Lancaster

240

said. "You did."

"Well, I pay attention."

"That's what I'm saying," Lancaster said. "And I'll bet you pay attention to what's going on in town."

"I try to."

"Then you know when strangers ride in."

Bodeen smiled. He had good looks, which wouldn't hurt him in an election. "I saw you ride in."

"So you're making my point even stronger for me," Lancaster said. "You know when strangers come to town, so you've seen the ones I'm looking for."

"I can't get to them all," Bodeen said. "That's the sheriff's job."

"So when Gerry Beck came through here, you either did or didn't see him."

"I may have seen him and not known his name."

Lancaster took the time to describe Beck. According to Andy Black's description, Beck hadn't changed very much since he'd last seen him.

"Guess that could be a lot of people," Bodeen said. He seemed annoyed to have to admit that Beck might have been in town without him knowing it.

"What about a man named Sweet? My description of him isn't so good."

241

"Sweet was here."

Lancaster sat forward. "You sure?"

"It ain't a common name."

"When?"

"A week, maybe ten days ago."

"With anybody?"

"No, he was alone."

"How do you know?"

"I braced him when he rode in," Bodeen said. "I could see he was trouble."

"How did he react to being braced?"

"Took it in stride," Bodeen said. "Seemed real calm. We talked in one of the other saloons. He didn't break a sweat."

"Did he say anything about waiting to meet anybody else?"

"No. I asked him what he was up to, but he said he was just passing through."

"And how long did he stay?"

"About six days, maybe a full week."

"And what did he do?"

"Sat in front of his hotel, walked around town, drank, gambled . . ."

"He was killing time."

"That's what I thought," Bodeen said. "Like he was waitin' for somebody, but they never showed up."

"And he finally left?"

"Just up and rode out," Bodeen said. "Never made any trouble."

242

"Could he have left a message for anyone?"

"Might've, but I don't know who."

"Where'd he stay?"

"Fifth Street Hotel, down the block."

"Do you know where he left his horse?"

"Livery over on South Street."

"Any place else?"

"Like where?"

"Whorehouse?"

Bodeen scratched his head, drank some beer. "I never saw him go to a whorehouse."

"Okay," Lancaster said. "When I got here I was trailing two riders. I figure they got here about three days ahead of me."

"What'd they look like?"

"Not sure," Lancaster said. "Just a couple of cowpokes who'd been in a fight recently — although any cuts or bruises might have healed by now."

"Like the one over your eye?"

"This was compliments of a kick to the head by Sweet," Lancaster said. "I owe him."

"So you're huntin' Beck for Wells Fargo, but Sweet's personal?"

"You've got it."

"And these other two?"

"They seem to know Sweet," Lancaster said. "I thought they might lead me to him."

"And they led you here."

"Yeah."

"Well, I might be able to help you with those two," Bodeen said.

"Yeah?"

"Drink up," Bodeen said. "I'll show you."

Lancaster pushed away his half-finished beer and said, "I'm ready now."

FIFTY-SIX

Bodeen led Lancaster to a rooming house down the street from the South Street Livery.

"They left their horses there," he said when they passed the livery.

"Same place as Sweet," Lancaster observed.

"That could be a coincidence," Bodeen said. "Most people use that one, or — where'd you leave your horse?"

Lancaster told him.

"Yeah, or that one."

When they got to the rooming house, Bodeen stopped across the street.

"Two men rode in three days ago, got a room there," he said.

"If we go to the livery and I look at their horses, I'll know," Lancaster said. "The liveryman in Flagstaff told me their horses need new shoes."

"Oh, they're the ones, all right."

245

"What makes you think they're the ones I followed?" Lancaster asked.

"Because when they got here, the first thing they did was start askin' around for Sweet."

"Why didn't you tell me that before?"

Bodeen shrugged. "I wanted to talk for a while."

"They in there now?"

Bodeen shrugged again. "I doubt it," he said. "They're usually out during the day."

"They go to one saloon over another?"

"They hit them all," Bodeen said.

"They must still be looking for Sweet," Lancaster said. "That means if Sweet did leave a message for them, they haven't gotten it yet."

"We could go lookin' for them."

"Or wait here for them to come back."

"That sounds boring," Bodeen said. " 'Sides, I got rounds to make."

"Okay," Lancaster said, "you have a point. It might be better for me to come back at night, when they're in their rooms. Who owns this place?"

"Feller named Winston."

Lancaster looked at him.

"I know, these places are usually run by women, widows."

"Older man?"

"Yeah, in his sixties. In fact . . ."

"What?"

"He's friends with the sheriff."

The two men who had tried to beat up Ray the bartender were in the Whiskey River Saloon, sulking over a couple of beers.

"The man tells us to meet him here, and then when we get here he ain't nowhere," Rafe Fielding complained.

"He probably had to leave," Lou Williams said. "I'm sure he woulda left us a message."

"Like where? With who?"

"How the hell am I supposed to know?" Williams asked. "He didn't know where we was gonna stay. Hell, we didn't know that till we got here. We just gotta keep lookin', otherwise we came all this way for nothin', didn't we?"

Fielding made a noise with his mouth.

"Get us two fresh beers," Williams said. "Then we'll check some of the other saloons."

"What about the whorehouses?" Fielding asked.

"Yeah," Williams said, "let's do that."

Sheriff Jacobs knocked on the door of the rooming house.

"I appreciate this, Sheriff," Lancaster said.

247

"Don't mention it," Jacobs said. "I'm just glad you and Bodeen talked about it."

"He doesn't check in with you about strangers?" Lancaster asked.

"I told you," Jacobs said, "he's ambitious. Keeps things to himself, hoping they'll do him some good."

"What's the story on this fella?" Lancaster asked.

"Frank Witt," Jacobs said. "Lost his wife, Ella, a few years ago, and she always wanted to run a rooming house. So he bought this one and runs it in her name."

When the door opened, a man Lancaster assumed was Witt looked out at them.

"Jimmy, what the hell? I didn't know you was droppin' by."

"Got some time, Frank?" Jacobs asked. "We'd like to talk about somethin'."

Witt looked at Lancaster, then back at Sheriff Jacobs.

"This fella is Lancaster," Jacobs said. "He needs some help."

"From me?"

"You and me," Jacobs said.

"Well, hell, sure, come on in," Witt said. "I got some good whiskey around here somewhere."

They followed Witt into a sitting room, where he pulled out a bottle of whiskey and three glasses.

"Not for me, thanks," Lancaster said.

"It's good stuff," Witt assured him.

"Probably too good," Lancaster said. "I used to be a drunk."

"Oh well . . . Jimmy?"

"Naw, I guess not, Frank," Jacobs said.

Witt reluctantly put the bottle away.

"Well," he said, "then just what is it I can do for you fellas?"

"You've got two boarders . . ." Jacobs started.

FIFTY-SEVEN

Fielding and Williams left the whorehouse, feeling satisfied in more ways than one.

"Why didn't we check these places before?" Williams asked.

"Just seemed to me Sweet would spend more time in a saloon."

"And maybe he did," Williams said, "but he left us a message with a whore."

"Probably figured that's where we'd spend most of our time," Fielding said.

Both men laughed.

"He probably woulda been right, if we hadn't been lookin' for his sorry ass all over creation," Fielding said.

"Wanna get a drink?" Williams asked.

"Naw," Fielding said. "Let's turn in and get an early start. Maybe we can catch up to him in a day or two."

"Yeah," Williams said, "okay."

They headed back to the rooming house.

■ ■ ■ ■

The two men entered the rooming house, both wanting nothing more than to get to their beds. They'd been drinking all day, and being with those whores had worn them out.

When they got to the main sitting room, though, they stopped. There were three men there. The only man they recognized was the old-timer who ran the place, but one of the other two was wearing a badge.

"What the hell —" Fielding said.

"Just stand easy, men," the sheriff said. "I'll need you to toss your guns on that sofa over there, and do it slow and easy."

"What's goin' on?" Williams asked.

"Just get rid of the iron and then we'll talk," Jacobs said. Lancaster stood ready, just in case the men tried to shoot it out. The rooming house owner stood off to one side, out of the way.

Williams and Fielding tossed their guns onto the sofa.

"Good," Jacobs said. "Frank here says your names are Fielding and Williams. That true?"

Fielding nodded.

"Which is which?"

"I'm Fielding," the man said.

"Okay, now we need to talk to you about a man called Sweet."

Both men stared at him.

Lancaster said, "The two of you jumped a bartender in Flagstaff, tried to give him a beating, but he fought back."

"We don't know what you're —"

"Don't even try it," Lancaster said. "We know it was you, and we know you were warning him about a man named Sweet."

"And we also know you came here to meet Sweet," Jacobs said. "He was here about a week ago, but now he's gone."

"Figure he left you a message, which you may or may not have already picked up."

Then two men looked at each other.

"I need to know where he is," Lancaster said. "I don't care about you two."

"You'll let us go?" Williams asked.

"That's right."

"I want him to say it," Fielding said, indicating the lawman.

"You ain't done nothin' here," Jacobs said. "At least, nothing that I know of. You give this feller what he wants and you can go. But you gotta get out of town."

"Tonight," Lancaster said.

"Tonight?" Williams whined. "Man, I'm beat —"

"We'll go," Fielding said. "We picked up Sweet's message tonight. He left it at the whorehouse with one of the whores."

"That's good," Lancaster said. "Now all you've got to do is tell me where he is."

"You gonna kill 'im?" Fielding asked.

"I just may do that," Lancaster said.

"Naw, you gotta kill 'im," Williams said. "If he finds out we gave him up he'll kill us."

"Don't worry," Lancaster said. "I'm gonna kill him."

"I didn't hear that," Sheriff Jacobs said. "You hear that, Frank?"

"I didn't hear a thing," Frank said.

"That good enough for you?" Lancaster asked the two men.

"That'll do," Fielding said.

Fifty-Eight

Jacobs put the two men in a jail cell.

"You said we had to leave town!" Fielding complained from inside his cell.

"You do."

"But you said tonight."

"Well, maybe I misspoke there," Jacobs said. "I'm just gonna keep ya here for a while, so you can't get to Sweet and warn him."

"We don't wanna warn Sweet," Fielding said. "We want you to kill 'im."

"I'm just makin' sure," the sheriff said. "Relax, I'll feed ya good and let ya out in a couple of days. Just consider yourselves my guests."

"Guests?" Williams asked, rattling the door of his cell. "With locked doors?"

"Don't want you to get out and hurt yerselves," Jacobs said.

He left the cell block, went out into the office where Lancaster was standing with

Deputy Bodeen.

"That was a good idea, Sheriff," Lancaster said. "I appreciate it."

"I just figured they might leave town and suddenly remember they're more afraid of Sweet than you," Jacobs said. "This'll give you time to catch up to Sweet yourself."

"Where did they say he is?" Bodeen asked.

Lancaster looked at the deputy and said, "The less people who know that, the better."

"You don't trust me?"

"It ain't that," Lancaster said. "I just want to keep it to myself for now. If I get there and Sweet's been warned, I don't want to have to wonder who told him."

"Nobody's gonna tell him," Bodeen said, "because these two are in jail and you ain't tellin' me. If he gets warned . . ." He trailed off.

"It would have to be by me, is that what you were gonna say?" Jacobs asked.

"Or Frank at the rooming house," Lancaster pointed out. "He was there to hear it, too. See? Already two people who know. I'm gonna keep it to myself, Deputy. Get insulted if you want, but there it is."

"Ah," the deputy said, waving his hand. "Do what you want, Lancaster. It's your business."

"That's right," Lancaster said. "It is."

"What about Beck?" Jacobs asked.

"I'll have to take care of Sweet first," Lancaster said, "and then find Beck."

"No word on him?" Bodeen asked.

"No."

"Think he knows Sweet?"

"We talked about that already," Lancaster said. "Too much of a coincidence."

"What about the man who hired Sweet and those other two?" Jacobs asked.

"I'm gonna have to find that out from Sweet."

"What if he won't tell you?" Bodeen asked.

"He'll tell me," Lancaster said.

"How can you be so sure?" the deputy asked.

"Because I'm gonna make it impossible for him not to tell me," Lancaster said.

Bodeen laughed and asked, "What are you gonna do, torture it out of him?"

Lancaster just stared at Bodeen, who looked at the sheriff.

"He is, isn't he?" he asked. "He's gonna torture him, and then kill him."

Sheriff Jacobs shrugged and said, "I didn't hear that."

256

FIFTY-NINE

Sweetwater, Texas

Fielding and Williams had told Lancaster that Sweet left them a message to meet him in Sweetwater. They also told him that Sweet had a bank job planned, but they weren't sure where it was. Could be Abilene, or maybe even Fort Worth.

Lancaster wondered about Sweet wanting to meet in Sweetwater. Did the man have that much of a sense of humor, or was the irony lost on him?

He rode into town, armed with a more accurate description of the man given him by Fielding. He hoped that when he saw Sweet he'd recognize him. The man's face was still a mystery in his memory of the events in the Mojave Desert. His brain was still trying to put it all together, which led to bad dreams that ended in him coming awake in a cold sweat. The doctor had said his memory might come back on its own, might not come back, or might return as the result of a shock.

He hoped that seeing Sweet's face would be that shock.

The man known as Sweet didn't use his first name. He hated it. He had once told a woman his name, and she had begun calling him that and he finally had to kill her to shut her up. Well, he also had to kill her so he wouldn't have to share the proceeds from a big robbery with her, but that was another story. The way she used his first name was reason enough to have killed her.

Sweet was sitting in a saloon in Sweetwater, wondering when those two idiots, Fielding and Williams, would show up. If they didn't get there in the next few days, he was going to have to try to find men someplace else. The payroll that was going to be in the Abilene bank would not be there forever. He couldn't afford to wait more than a few more days.

The furthest thing from his mind at that moment was what had happened to Lancaster in the Mojave Desert. That was just an old job at the back of his mind and it never occurred to him to wonder about Lancaster, or about his two partners in that job. He was only looking ahead to future jobs.

■ ■ ■ ■

Lancaster decided to keep a low profile. He was not going to ask questions in any of the saloons, and he wasn't going to consult with the local law. He didn't want to ask anybody about a man named Sweet. He was just going to look for him himself.

But Sweetwater was not a small town, and he knew a horse like Crow Bait would attract attention on the street, so he had to get him into the livery.

"That horse got you here?" the man in the livery asked.

"He's done a lot more than that," Lancaster said, dismounting. "And don't talk about him to anybody. I hear you been bad-mouthing this horse and I'll be back to see you."

"Hey," the man said, eyes wide, "I won't say a word, mister."

"See that you don't," Lancaster said. "And take good care of him."

"I will, I swear."

Lancaster pointed his finger at the man one more time before taking his saddlebags and rifle and walking out.

He deliberately got himself a room in the smallest hotel in town. He left his rifle and saddlebags there, and then hit the street to start his search for Sweet.

Along the way he came across a small café and went inside for a bite to eat. The waiter was a quiet, middle-aged man who didn't talk beyond asking him what he wanted, which suited Lancaster fine.

Lancaster did something he usually never did — sat at the window. He wanted to watch the street while he ate. Maybe Sweet would simply cross in front of him, making it easy to find him.

And maybe not.

He finished eating, then went back out to walk the town and check the saloons.

The Texas and Pacific Railroad had come through Sweetwater in 1883, and the town had grown since then to the point where it had five saloons and many other businesses. As far as he was able to tell, though, having walked through the town one time, there was no whorehouse. There might have been whores in the saloons, but he didn't see a houseful of them.

He checked three of the saloons, preferring to peer in over the batwing doors rather than go in and have a beer at each of them. If he did that he'd be in no shape when he finally found Sweet.

When he got to the fourth saloon, a place

called Del's Saloon, he looked in the window, saw a man sitting alone at a table, and stared.

Was that him?

He moved to the batwing doors to get a better look. With the description from Fielding, this certainly looked like Sweet, but what if Fielding had been lying?

Lancaster decided to take a chance and walk into the saloon. Maybe Sweet would see him and recognize him. He knew if he had kicked a man half to death and left him to die in the desert, he would remember him.

The saloon was less than half-full, and Lancaster was able to belly up to the bar without having to attract attention.

"Beer," he said to the bartender.

"Comin' up."

The man put a full mug in front of him, but Lancaster wasn't paying attention. He had his head turned and was looking at the man at the table. Suddenly, as if he knew he was being watched, the man raised his head and their eyes met.

Lancaster felt the shock he'd been waiting for as he saw the man's face.

SIXTY

It all came back to him.

He remembered his horse being shot and then the three men were on him. Sweet was the most brutal. Kicking him repeatedly when he was down, kicking him that last time as one of the other men called Sweet by name.

"Sweet, don't . . ."

Lancaster noticed another thing, too, as their eyes met.

There was no recognition in Sweet's face at all. He stared at Lancaster for a moment; then he turned his eyes down again, staring into his drink.

The man had no idea who he was, and so he also had no idea what was about to happen.

Lancaster took one sip from his beer, then turned and walked over to Sweet's table, carrying the beer in his left hand.

"Sweet."

Sweet looked up as he heard his name. He stared at Lancaster, and even this close he didn't show any trace of recognition.

"I know you?"

"You should."

Sweet took a moment; then he said, "Well, I don't, so get lost."

"Afraid I can't do that," Lancaster said.

Sweet looked up at him again. "You lookin' for trouble, friend?"

"Well, I wasn't," Lancaster said. "I was just minding my own business when you and your buddies jumped me in the desert and left me to die."

"What the hell are you — wait a minute." Sweet squinted. "Lancaster?"

"That's right, Sweet," Lancaster said. "Mind if I join you?"

He didn't wait for a response. He pulled out the chair across from the man and sat down.

"How the hell —"

"Never thought you'd see me again, did you?"

"You should be dead," Sweet said. "I shoulda killed you, but —"

"But you weren't being paid to kill me, right?" Lancaster asked. "You were being paid to leave me afoot in the desert with no water and no gun."

263

"You know that?"

"I remembered just enough to know that the three of you were being paid."

"So there's no hard feelin's, right?" Sweet said. "It was just a job."

"Oh no, I can't agree with you there, Sweet," Lancaster said. "I've got lots of hard feelings, for you and your partners. But see . . . they're already dead, so that leaves you."

"They're dead?"

"Yes."

Sweet licked his lips.

"B-but they couldn't tell you who hired us," he said. "Only I know that."

"And you're gonna tell me, right?"

"Well," Sweet said, a crafty look coming into his eyes, "maybe we can make a deal."

SIXTY-ONE

"What kind of a deal?" Lancaster asked.

"I'll tell you who hired me, and you let me go," Sweet said. "Simple as that."

"I've got a counteroffer."

"What's that?"

"You tell me who hired you," Lancaster said, "and I'll kill you quickly."

Sweet rocked back in his chair. "That's a joke, right?"

"No joke," Lancaster said. "Make no mistake, Sweet. There's no way you walk away from this alive. Not after what you did to me. But how you die, well, that's up for discussion."

"How about this?" Sweet asked. "Why don't I just kill you right now?"

"Do it," Lancaster said. "Go ahead. With your hands? Your gun? Or do you plan to kick me to death?"

Sweet stared at Lancaster.

"That's what I thought," Lancaster said.

"You don't have two more men to back your play this time."

"Look, I told you already," Sweet said. "It weren't nothin' personal. We was hired to do what we did."

"And you're gonna tell me by who and why."

"Well," Sweet said, "you got somebody mad at you, that's for sure. Had somethin' to do with somebody you killed."

"So, what? Somebody's wife? Somebody's father? Brother?" Lancaster asked.

"I don't know," Sweet said. "To tell you the truth, I didn't care. It was a lot of money."

"And how specific was this person when they hired you?" Lancaster asked.

"Whataya mean?"

"Why the Mojave?"

"That's what . . . they wanted," Sweet said. "For us to strand you in the middle of the Mojave. They said take your horse, your gun, your water, and leave you."

"And you didn't ask why?"

Sweet shrugged. "Like I said, it was a lot of money."

"But you didn't leave me right in the middle of the desert," Lancaster said. "If you had I might be dead now."

"Well, I didn't see any reason to wait,"

Sweet said.

"You got impatient," Lancaster said. "You hadn't been paid yet, right?"

"Not all of it."

"So after you left me you had to go and meet your employer to get paid. That means he or she was in Nevada, right?"

"So?"

"But do they live in Nevada?"

Sweet didn't answer.

"Sweet," Lancaster said, "the harder you make this on me, the harder it's gonna be on you."

"Naw," Sweet said, "naw, you ain't gonna kill me. Not while you don't know who hired me."

"And if you're so bound and determined not to tell me," Lancaster asked, "what's the point of me keepin' you alive?"

Sweet stared at Lancaster, then picked up his drink — whiskey, by the look of it — and swigged it.

"I ain't just gonna lie down for you, Lancaster," he said.

"I never thought you would," Lancaster said. "But why cover for your employer? You'll be dead and they'll go on living."

"And when they find out you're still alive, they'll hire somebody else," Sweet said. "You'll be lookin' over your shoulder for the rest of your life. You don't want me, Lancaster. You want who hired me."

Lancaster gave that some thought. Sweet began to look hopeful. He didn't think he had much chance going up against Lancaster in a fair gunfight. There had to be another way out. He looked at the batwing doors, hoping to see Fielding and Williams come through.

"Don't be lookin' for them," Lancaster said.

"For who?"

"Fielding and Williams," he said. "They're in a cell in Amarillo."

"Goddamnit!" Sweet said.

"Okay," Lancaster said. "Okay, Sweet."

"Okay, what?"

"You're right," Lancaster said. "I want the person who hired you."

"And?"

"Tell me who hired you," Lancaster said, "and I'll let you walk out that door."

Sweet looked hopeful, then suspicious.

"Oh no," he said, "you gotta be more plain than that. You let me walk out, then you come out and shoot me. Huh-uh. I want you to say it. If I tell you the name, you'll let me go."

"If you give me the name of the person who hired you, I'll let you go."

"And you won't come huntin' for me again."

"And I won't come huntin' for you again."

"And you won't ever kill me."

Lancaster hesitated; then he said, "And I won't ever kill you."

Sweet still looked suspicious.

"This is too easy," he said.

"Hey," Lancaster said, "what can I say? You convinced me."

Lancaster left the saloon with the name of the person who had hired Sweet to strand him in the desert. He also had the location.

He hated letting Sweet go, but he actually believed that the man would take his employer's name to the grave just to be ornery.

He still had to find Gerry Beck. But even Gerry was going to have to wait until Lancaster settled with the person who paid to have him left in the desert.

The problem was, he thought that once he heard the name he'd know who it was. But even armed with the name, he had no idea who the hell this person was.

SIXTY-TWO

Just outside Reno, Nevada

Lancaster had checked the ranch out in the daylight. It had a lot of hands, but at this time of night they were all in the bunkhouse. He had left Crow Bait in a stand of trees a few hundred yards away and come the rest of the way on foot.

He would like to have observed the place longer, but he didn't have the time. He didn't want to hang around Reno too long. Word might get back to the ranch. No, he had to go in tonight.

He worked his way to the back of the house without being seen and found a door that led to the kitchen. In daylight he'd been able to see that the house was a two-story Colonial with white columns in front, based on the mansions of the Deep South. A man with a house like this had to have servants — a cook, a maid, probably a manservant of some kind. He also might have had a wife

270

and some children. But at the moment the kitchen looked dark and deserted.

He tried the door and found it locked, but with a little pressure from his shoulder it gave and he was in.

Once inside, he drew his gun and moved to the doorway. It led to a dining room, also dark and empty. He had chosen to hit the house at two A.M., feeling that any family would be asleep.

He moved across the dining room to the entry hall, and noticed that there was a light burning on the first floor of the house, at the end of a hall.

He looked upstairs, at the darkness there. Upstairs, family members might have been asleep in their beds, including the man he was looking for. But he decided to check the light out first.

As quietly as he could he moved across the hardwood floor to the hallway, toward the room with the light. It was probably the rancher's office. If that was the case, then his search was over.

He stepped into the doorway, pointing his gun into the room. The figure behind the desk looked up at him in surprise.

"Who are you?" the girl asked.

"I could ask you the same thing."

"But I live here," she said. "You don't."

"Good point."

He looked back up the hallway, then stepped into the room, holding his gun down at his side.

"What's your name?" he asked.

"Angie," she said. "What's yours?"

"Lancaster. How old are you, Angie?"

"I'm fourteen, so don't go thinkin' I'm just a kid."

"I wouldn't do that," Lancaster said.

"Are you here to steal?" she asked.

"No."

"Then what are you doin' in my house?"

"I'm looking for a man named Roger Simon. Do you know him?"

"Of course," she said. "He's my father. He's upstairs asleep."

"With your mother?"

"No," she said. "My mother's dead."

"Oh, I'm sorry. How did it happen?"

"A man killed her," she said.

"When did that happen?"

"Last year. Are you here to hurt my dad?"

"No, Angie," he said. "I'm here to talk to him. Why don't you go up and tell him I'm here?"

"He'll be mad that I was in his office."

"Honey," Lancaster said, "I guarantee you he won't be mad."

SIXTY-THREE

Lancaster was sitting behind the desk in the room when Roger Simon appeared in the doorway. He was a tall, handsome man with steel gray hair and a strong jaw. The position of his hands revealed something to Lancaster.

"If you got a gun stuck in your belt behind you, Simon, I wouldn't go for it." Lancaster touched his own gun, which was on the desk.

Simon's hands twitched, as if he was surprised at Lancaster's words.

"Where's your daughter?" Lancaster asked.

"She's upstairs," Simon said. "You leave her alone."

Lancaster had no intention of hurting the girl, but he said, "That'll be up to you. Take the gun out and drop it in the hall."

Simon hesitated, then reached behind him, produced the gun, and dropped it on

273

the floor outside the room.

"Now come on in and sit down," Lancaster said. "We need to talk."

"You're not here to kill me?" There was no fear in the man's voice, just curiosity.

"Again," Lancaster said, "that'll be up to you."

Simon came forward and sat down.

"What do you want?" he demanded.

"I want to know why you hired three men to attack me and leave me to die in the desert?"

"You don't know?" Simon asked.

"I have no idea," Lancaster said. "I don't even know you. Never heard your name until Sweet told me."

"Sweet? Did you kill him?"

"I traded him his life for your name."

Simon firmed his jaw.

"The other two men who were with him are dead." Lancaster didn't bother to point out he hadn't killed them himself.

"Well?" Lancaster asked.

"Well what?"

"If you want to save your life, start talking," Lancaster said. "Why did you pay three men to kill me?"

"You're saying you really don't know?"

"I'm saying I have no idea!"

"My wife was killed last year, in the Mo-

274

jave Desert," Simon said. "She was on a stagecoach with several other people when the coach was robbed. The horses were driven off, and the passengers were left on foot. My wife was not a well woman, and she did not survive the trek through the desert." His eyes filled with tears. "She died out there."

"What the hell has that got to do with me?"

"I paid a lot of money to find out who the leader of that gang was," Simon said.

"And you came up with my name?"

"Like I said," Simon offered, "I paid a lot of money for the information."

"So because you paid a lot you believed it?" Lancaster asked. "Did you bother to check it out?"

"I investigated your background," Simon said. "You were a gun for hire for a long time."

"So that makes me a stage robber?" Lancaster asked. "Simon, I think maybe you wanted information so bad you were an easy target for some dangerous lies."

Simon stared at Lancaster, but the expression on his face said he wasn't so confident anymore that he'd paid for the correct information.

"Y-you can't prove that you didn't do it,"

the man stammered.

"Sure I can," Lancaster said. "You tell me when it happened and I bet I can prove I was elsewhere. But the proof may simply be in the name of the person who sold you the information."

Simon swallowed with difficulty.

"Who was it?" Lancaster asked. "What was his name?"

Simon started to speak; then he realized Lancaster was probably right. He licked his lips.

"Let me guess," Lancaster said. "The man who sold you the information was Sweet."

Simon nodded jerkily.

"Then after you paid him for that, he negotiated a price to take care of me for you."

Simon nodded again.

At that point Angie appeared in the doorway, holding her dad's gun with both hands and pointing it at Lancaster.

"Let my dad go!" she said.

Simon turned and his face paled as he saw his daughter.

"D-don't —" he stammered, holding his hand out to Lancaster. "Don't kill her —"

"I don't intend to kill your daughter, Simon," Lancaster said, "but you better talk

276

to her before she pulls that trigger and ruins
her life — and mine."

277

SIXTY-FOUR

Ardmore, Oklahoma, one month later

As Lancaster rode Crow Bait into Ardmore, he thought that he and the horse were finally together, in body and in mind. His memory had returned completely, his injuries were healed, he had returned everything he'd borrowed to Mal in Laughlin, but in the end he had not been able to give up the horse. He had his own rig — saddle, saddlebags, horse, and holster — and even Crow Bait's bones weren't sticking out quite as much as they had been.

Ardmore was small, hardly more than a stopover between Oklahoma City and Fort Worth. But that was okay, because Lancaster only meant to stop over.

Since the night Roger Simon had successfully disarmed his teenage daughter, Lancaster had devoted his time to tracking Gerry Beck for Wells Fargo. He'd managed to convince Simon he had nothing to do with

278

his wife's death. Simon had then tried to hire Lancaster to kill Sweet, but with no success. And Lancaster had tried to convince him not to hire anyone else, either.

"Men like Sweet usually get what's coming to them, Mr. Simon," he'd said.

He didn't know if Simon believed him, but it didn't matter. He was done with the whole deal. His concern became collecting that other four thousand dollars from Wells Fargo.

He reined in Crow Bait in front of the saloon, dismounted, and tied him off there.

"Jesus," an old man said from the boardwalk, "looks like he's on his last legs."

"His legs are just fine," Lancaster said. "Don't you worry about it."

He had long ago overcome the urge to shoot anybody who criticized the horse. None of them knew what they were talking about, anyway.

He mounted the boardwalk and entered the saloon. He looked around, noticed a few of the other tables were taken. He collected a beer from the bar and walked to a table near the back of the room.

"Mind if I join you?" he asked.

Gerry Beck looked up at him, frowning. "Lancaster? What the hell are you doin' here?"

"Right now I'm just looking for someplace to sit and drink my beer."

"Well, find someplace else to do it."

"Naw," Lancaster said, sitting down, "I'll do it here."

Beck sat back and stared at him.

"What the hell —" he said.

"It's been a while, Gerry."

"Yeah," Beck said, "and if I remember right, you and me were never friends, so get lost."

"I can't," Lancaster said. "I promised Wells Fargo I'd bring you in."

"Bounty hunting now?" Beck asked.

"Not exactly."

"Well, what, exactly?"

"I just sort of found myself in a situation where I had to take the job."

"The job of bringin' me in?"

Lancaster nodded.

"Well, it ain't gonna be easy," Beck told him. "I hope they paid you enough."

"Don't get paid until the job is done," Lancaster said.

"Well, then," Beck said with a steely grin, "I guess you ain't gettin' paid, are you."

"Oh, I'll get paid," he said, pushing half his beer away. "So, how many men you got in here backing you up, Gerry?"

"What?"

"I know your style, Gerry," Lancaster said. "You don't go anywhere or do anything without someone to back you up. Let's see."

Lancaster looked around the room. There were five other men there, four sitting at tables, two of them looking back at him.

"My guess is these two, one to my left, one to my right. But I also know you don't pay well, so they won't be very good."

"Good enough to get you before you get me," Beck said, "or to keep you busy while I get you."

"No," Lancaster said. "I think I'll have to get you first, and then them. Only once you're dead, they may not be so anxious to skin their irons, will they?"

Beck stared at Lancaster, trying to make up his mind. But Lancaster had already made up his.

"Sorry," he said, drawing his gun and standing up.

Beck tried to react, but he was too slow. Lancaster shot him in the chest, then overturned the table and dropped down behind it.

The other two men stood, drawing their guns, while everyone else in the saloon hit the floor.

They fired, the bullets taking chunks out of the overturned table.

Lancaster rolled the table one way; then he rolled the other. Not being the smartest men Beck could have hired, they kept firing at the table. Lancaster fired two well-placed shots and suddenly it was quiet.

He walked over to where Beck lay dead and said, "Should have hired better help, Gerry."

SIXTY-FIVE

Laughlin, Nevada, two months later
Crow Bait was dying.

Lancaster could feel it beneath him.

Whatever energy had been driving the gallant animal since they'd met was waning away.

Mal came out of the stable and watched as they rode toward him.

"Now he really is on his last legs, isn't he?" Mal asked as horse and rider reached him.

Lancaster dismounted and walked the horse over to Mal. "You can see it?"

"Oh yes."

Lancaster rubbed the animal's neck.

"Did you get done everything you had to get done?" Mal asked.

"Almost."

He handed the reins to Mal.

"I wish I was smart enough to study him," Mal said, patting the animal on his flank, "find out what made him go."

"Do what you can for him," Lancaster said.

"I'll keep him alive and comfortable as long as I can," Mal said. "Well, at least he got you back here, where it started."

"What good does that do me?"

"Well, he's here," Mal said. "I've actually been waitin' for you."

"What? Who's here?"

"Sweet."

"What?"

"Yeah," Mal said. "Came back here. Guess he figured this is the last place you'd look. Now you can finish him."

Lancaster hesitated; then he said, "I can't."

"Why not?"

"I made a deal with him," he said. "Promised I wouldn't hunt for him anymore."

"But you didn't hunt for him," Mal said. "You just came back here, and here he was. Or is."

Lancaster thought a moment. "Good point. But I also promised I'd never kill him."

Mal smiled. "You'll figure somethin' out."

Hours later Lancaster reined in the two horses he'd borrowed from Mal.

"This ain't right," Sweet said. "You promised."

Lancaster looked at Sweet. He'd hauled the man out of a saloon and tied him to a horse. Now they were out in the Mojave, farther out than they'd been when Sweet left him to die.

"You said you wouldn't hunt me," Sweet reminded him.

"I didn't. I came back to Laughlin, and you were there."

"I never believed you," Sweet said. "Thought you'd come lookin' for me."

"And figured Laughlin would be the last place I would look," Lancaster said. "And you were right. Imagine my surprise."

Lancaster dismounted and started to untie Sweet's hands.

"B-but you promised you'd never kill me."

"I'm not going to kill you," Lancaster said.

When one of Sweet's hands was free, he couldn't wait. He swung at Lancaster, who blocked it and yanked the man from the saddle. Sweet hit the ground hard, all the air going out of him. Lancaster thought about kicking him a few times, but decided against it. Instead, he got back on his horse.

Sweet rolled onto his ass and looked up at Lancaster. "You ain't gonna leave me here with no water."

"Sure I am."

"I'll never make it."

"Maybe you'll find a miracle in the desert," Lancaster said. "I did."

"I don't believe in miracles," Sweet said.

"Too bad. Oh, one more thing."

"Wh-what?"

"Toss your boots up here."

Lancaster came out of the telegraph office and found Mal waiting for him.

"Get your message off?" Mal asked.

"Yes," Lancaster said. "Roger Simon will soon know that the man who killed his wife is gone."

"Any chance he can walk out?" Mal asked.

"None," Lancaster said. "That's the advantage I had of having been through it before. How's Crow Bait?"

"Resting comfortably," Mal said. "I figured out he's old — real old."

"But you'll take care of him."

"Oh yeah."

Lancaster had had a good night's sleep since returning from the Mojave. Now, with the telegram sent, he was finally free of everything that had begun that day in the desert.

Now he had only one thought.

"Buy you breakfast?" he asked Mal. "I've

got a lot of Wells Fargo money left."

"Sounds good to me."